"Hello, Jen," Michael said without turning around.

Jen moved to stand beside him. "How did you know I was behind you?"

"I think there are some people in this world that others are simply aware of."

"In general terms?"

"Oh, no," he said quietly. "In very specific terms." He turned his head and looked at her for a long moment. "I just know where you are without having to see you."

Their eyes locked. Things had changed between them since their first meeting. In fact, things had changed dramatically since last night. They were both aware of each other in new ways.

Ways they shouldn't be.

Ways they needed to avoid.

Dear Reader,

What would July be without fun in the sun, dazzling fireworks displays—or heartwarming love stories from the Special Edition line? Romance seems even more irresistible in the balmy days of summer, and our six books for this month are sure to provide hours of reading pleasure.

This July, Myrna Temte continues her HEARTS OF WYOMING series with an engaging story about best friends turned lovers. THAT SPECIAL WOMAN! Alexandra McBride Talbot is determined not to get involved with her handsome next-door neighbor, but he goes to extraordinary lengths to win this single mom's stubborn heart in *Urban Cowboy*.

Sometimes true love knows no rhyme or reason. Take for instance the headstrong heroine in *Hannah and the Hellion* by Christine Flynn. Everyone warned this sweetheart away from the resident outcast, but she refused to abandon the rogue of her dreams. Or check out the romance-minded rancher who's driven to claim the heart of his childhood crush in *The Cowboy's Ideal Wife* by bestselling author Victoria Pade—the next installment in her popular A RANCHING FAMILY series. And Martha Hix's transformation story proves how love can give a gruff, emotionally scarred hero a new lease on life in *Terrific Tom*.

Rounding off the month, we've got *The Sheik's Mistress* by Brittany Young—a forbidden-love saga about a soon-to-be betrothed sheik and a feisty American beauty. And pure, platonic friendship turns into something far greater in *Baby Starts the Wedding March* by Amy Frazier.

I hope you enjoy each and every story to come!

Sincerely,

Tara Gavin,
Editorial Manager

Please address questions and book requests to:
Silhouette Reader Service
U.S.: 3010 Walden Ave., P.O. Box 1325, Buffalo, NY 14269
Canadian: P.O. Box 609, Fort Erie, Ont. L2A 5X3

BRITTANY YOUNG

THE SHEIK'S MISTRESS

Published by Silhouette Books

America's Publisher of Contemporary Romance

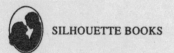

SILHOUETTE BOOKS

ISBN 0-373-24187-9

THE SHEIK'S MISTRESS

This edition published by arrangement with Harlequin Books S.A.

Printed in U.S.A.

BRITTANY YOUNG

lives and writes in Racine, Wisconsin. She has traveled to most of the countries that serve as the settings for her books and finds the research into the language, customs, history and literature of these countries among the most demanding and rewarding aspects of her writing.

RULES OF A SHEIK'S MISTRESS:

1. Do not be intimidated by his intense appraisal, his feral need to protect, his possessive caress.

2. Do speak your mind—sure, he's a king, but at heart he is a man.

3. Do welcome his touch in the dark of night when there are no rules, no restrictions... only passion.

4. Never forget he is betrothed to another.

5. Avoid falling in love at all costs.

THE JEN O'HARA CLAUSE:

After following the above and still losing your heart, make that sheik yearn for your laugh, your love—and, against all odds, your hand in marriage.

Chapter One

Jensen stood in front of the Sumaru airport, just miles from the capital city of Sumara, set seemingly right in the middle of the Sahara Desert, and waited. Heat rose lazily from the pavement and washed over her in nauseating waves. She'd never felt heat like this; never breathed heat like this. It was suffocating.

A man in long white robes and traditional head-dress walked past her carrying a briefcase, rudely eyeing her up and down. Jensen was tall and long legged, with nearly waist length blond hair pulled straight away from her heat-flushed face into a thick ponytail. Those legs were bare, as were her arms. And even though the blue sundress was modestly cut with a fairly full skirt that hit just above her knees, the man made her feel as though she were naked.

She stared back at him with narrowed green eyes that silently challenged him.

It had no effect.

She should have read up on this place before coming here. It was clear she was going to be crashing into thousand-year-old customs and traditions all over the place.

Of course, if it weren't for her brother Henry, she wouldn't have to be here at all.

Henry.

Jensen sank onto the edge of her largest suitcase while she waited for a taxi to show up.

She was so angry with him.

And frightened.

Was it only two days earlier that she'd been sitting peacefully in her renovated Wisconsin farmhouse with its vast green lawn and even its own small lake set in the forest....

Jensen wiped the beads of sweat from her forehead with the back of her hand. That sounded like paradise at the moment.

She could still hear her housekeeper's voice calling through the door of her home office to tell her there was a telephone call she should take. Jensen looked around. The call that would bring her to this forsaken place in the middle of nowhere....

"Jen?" said the housekeeper as she knocked on the closed door. "Sorry to disturb you, dear. I know you're trying to finish your book, but there's a telephone call and it sounds important."

Jensen O'Hara typed a few more words into her computer. "That's all right, Mrs. Sherman. I'll get it.'' She reached over and punched the speaker button on the phone. "Hello," she said absently, still looking at her computer screen.

"Ms. O'Hara?" asked a foreign-sounding voice.

"Yes?"

"I have some news of your brother."

That got her attention. Her brother had been in the Middle East working on a story for his magazine for more than a month. Two weeks earlier he'd called her to say he was coming to Wisconsin to visit her between stories but hadn't yet shown up. That wasn't all that unusual. Henry could be fairly unreliable when it came to time. In fact, he seemed to have no sense of it at all. So when a few days had gone by and there was no Henry, Jensen wasn't too concerned.

Then the few days turned into a week, and Jensen had begun to get really worried. She hadn't tried to track him down, though. Not at that point. The last time she'd done that, he'd given her a lecture that had left her ears ringing.

Now two weeks had passed and, lecture or not, she'd started making phone calls in an effort to find him. She had a very bad feeling about this, and if there was one thing Jensen had learned over the years, it was to trust her feelings.

She grabbed the receiver and held it to her ear. "What about Henry? Has something happened?"

"He seems to have disappeared."

"What?"

"We can't find him."

"We who? Who are you?"

"My apologies. I'm with the American Embassy in the country of Sumaru, city of Sumara."

"It took you long enough to return my calls!"

"We wanted to do some investigating before contacting you."

"What did you find out?"

"He was indeed in the city, staying at the Metropole Hotel. He checked out approximately five days ago without saying where he was headed."

"Then he should have been on his way to Wisconsin."

"Perhaps he is."

"Sir, he most certainly would have arrived by now if that were the case. He's not exactly traveling here by camel. Did you check the outbound airline passenger lists?"

"Of course."

"And?"

"His name wasn't on any of them."

"So he's still in Sumaru."

"We don't think so. No one has seen him. It's entirely possible he left by car and departed from some other city."

"Why would he do that? He told me he was coming here directly from Sumaru."

"Your brother is a journalist, Miss O'Hara. They're known to follow stories. He did, in fact, suggest that very thing to some people at the hotel."

"What people?"

"The gentleman who checked him out of his room, for one."

Jensen shook her head. "Henry knew I was expecting him. He would have called me if that were the case.''

''I suggest you call his employer.''

Jensen dragged her fingers through her hair. ''The magazine was the first place I called. They said he was due in New York this past week and didn't show up.''

''I don't know what else to tell you, miss. There's nothing more we can do from this end.''

''But...''

''I'm sorry we couldn't be of more help.''

The line went dead before she could say anything else.

Jensen hung up the phone and just sat there. She had to do something. Call someone.

Even as she had the thought, the phone rang again.

She grabbed it. ''Listen,'' she said, thinking she was speaking to the man from the embassy, ''you can't just proclaim that my brother has dropped from the face of the earth—your country to be precise— and leave it at that.''

''Is this Miss O'Hara? Miss Jensen O'Hara?'' asked a voice that definitely didn't belong to the previous caller.

''Yes,'' she said, her voice echoing her uncertainty. ''Who's this?''

''Let's just say I'm a friend of your brother's. You don't need to know any more than that.''

''You know Henry? Do you know where he is?''

''I can tell you that he isn't where he's supposed to be.''

"What does that mean?"

"He's not running down a story. He's missing."

"How do you know this?"

"I have my sources."

"You're not telling me anything," said Jensen as she stood up, too agitated to stay seated any longer. "Is Henry safe?"

"The answer to all of your questions are in Sumaru. All you have to do is go there."

"And if I don't?"

"Your brother might be lost to you forever."

"Is that a threat? Do you have Henry? Is it money you're after? I have some. Not a lot…"

The line went dead.

Jensen stared at it for a moment, then quickly started rummaging through her desk drawers. Her brother used her office sometimes when he visited. The last time, he'd left his address book behind.

She found it and quickly opened it to the page that listed Henry's best friend from college, Michael Hassan. Michael lived somewhere in Sumaru, though she understood he was an engineer and worked all over the world. Henry had mentioned that he might look up Michael before leaving the country.

She pressed the numbers and waited through fifteen seconds of silence before there was a ring.

A man answered in Arabic.

"Do you speak English?" asked Jensen.

"Yes."

"Thank heavens. I need to speak with Michael Hassan."

"I'm sorry but he is not available for telephone calls."

"This is really important. Perhaps if you tell him it's Henry O'Hara's sister calling from America, he'd take the call."

"He is taking no calls at this time."

Jensen sighed. There seemed to be no way through the man's cool formality. "May I leave a message?"

"If that is your wish."

"Please tell him that Henry was in Sumaru but appears to be missing. It's urgent that I speak with Michael to find out what he knows and whether or not he can help. Have him call me at home any time of the day or night. If I'm not here, my housekeeper will know where to find me." She gave him the number.

"I'll give him the message."

"Thank you."

As soon as she hung up, Jensen started calling the magazine and anyone else she could think of who might be able to help track Henry down.

And to make arrangements for her own flight to Sumaru.

So here she was, a woman who lived a basically cloistered life writing about other people's lives, who had never really been anywhere except through those characters, here, in this place.

Talk about being thrown in at the deep end of the pool.

Good grief.

Henry was going to pay dearly for this when she found him.

Bang!

Jensen jumped at the loud report and turned her head to locate the source of the backfire. Her heart sank when she saw the rusting hulk of a thirty-year-old taxi grinding its way noisily toward her. The sideview mirror on the passenger side dangled precariously by a wire. What appeared to have once been a vinyl roof was now nothing but sun-bleached flakes. Choking black exhaust billowed from its tailpipe.

It stopped at the curb in front of her and a young man in Western dress came bounding energetically out. "You come with me lady, okay?"

Jensen looked from the skinny, black-haired boy who appeared to be no more than thirteen to the rusting disaster of a taxi he'd pulled up in. "I don't think so," she said politely.

"You have to. It's your turn for ride, my turn for pick up. You come with me." His face was split by an utterly infectious smile as he reached for her luggage.

Jensen put her hand on her suitcase to stop him from lifting it. "How old are you?"

"Sixteen."

"And how long have you been sixteen?"

"Two weeks. Big party. Lots of people."

Jensen's mouth twitched into an involuntary smile. "Is this your taxi?"

"No, no. My uncle's. He's sick today, so I take over."

"How long have you been driving?"

"Since this morning. Early."

"No. I mean how old were you when you started driving?"

"Oh, yes, yes. Sorry. Ten," he said proudly. "My uncle taught me. He very great man."

"I'm sure he is."

"So you come now."

She reluctantly took away her hand and let him heave her suitcase into the trunk, then watched as he fastened the trunk lid closed with a narrow rope.

Oh, God.

She reached for the door handle, but the boy brushed her hand away. "No, no. I get it."

The door opened with a loud creak. She took a deep breath and climbed inside. The interior wasn't much better than the exterior, but it was clean.

The boy closed the door, walked quickly around the car and hopped—that's the only word Jensen could think of to describe it—onto the driver's seat. Turning around he grinned at her. "Where you want me take you?"

"The Metropole Hotel in Sumara. Do you know where that is?"

"Yusef," he said, apparently referring to himself, "know where everything is. You see. I get you there fast."

"I don't need fast. I just want to arrive in one piece," she said as she automatically gripped the armrest on the door.

"No problem, lady."

He pulled away from the curb and moved into the stream of traffic. "So where you from, lady?"

"Wisconsin."

"I don't know this place."

"It's next to Illinois," she explained, her watchful eye on the traffic.

He shook his head.

"Near Chicago."

"Chicago!" he said with the enthusiasm of recognition. "Al Capone. Bang, bang."

"Well, old Scarface has been gone for a while, but I think bang, bang still applies."

Even as Jensen spoke the words, the muffler fired a shot into the air.

"Why you here?" he asked. "Vacation?"

Jensen looked at her dusty, dry, beige surroundings. "Vacation? Here? I don't think so."

"So why you come?"

"I'm looking for my brother."

"He here on vacation?"

"You have a thing about people vacationing here, don't you? No. He was here working for a magazine and he disappeared."

"Oh, that's very bad. So you come look for him."

"Exactly."

"You know, woman alone not good here."

He abruptly cut in front of someone on the highway. Jensen closed her eyes.

"I had to come alone," she said. "But I know someone here. I'm sure he'll help me."

"Maybe Yusef can help."

"I don't think so, but thanks for offering."

"I know people."

"I'm sure you do, Yusef."

"I help you anyway."

Jensen left it alone. He'd no doubt forget about her as soon as he dropped her off if she didn't make an issue of it, she thought as she gazed out the window.

The four-lane highway seemed newly built. It was in wonderful condition. On either side was desert, but homes and businesses sat not far off the road, all of them swathed in great black cloths.

"What does the black mean?" she asked Yusef.

"Our great sheik and his oldest son were killed in plane crash one month ago. We are a country in mourning."

"I'm so sorry. Who will be sheik now?"

"The younger son is."

"Is that good or bad?"

"We don't know yet. Some think he's spent too much time in America. He's fond of Western ways." Yusef glanced at her in his rearview mirror. "My apologies, but Americans aren't very well thought of here, and we are more tolerant than most countries because our beloved Queen was American."

"Was?"

"She died many years ago."

"Is the younger son king now?"

"Yes. He became such the moment his father and brother died. But we have had no formal celebration yet."

"Of course." Jensen looked at the back of the

collar of his shirt. "You don't seem to mind West-
erners too much."

"Oh," he said with a big smile. "I love America.
Someday I go there. I will be a cowboy. Do you
have cowboys in Chicago?"

"Not real ones."

"Where are the real ones?"

Jensen thought for a moment. "Texas, I suppose.
Montana. Maybe Wyoming."

"Then that's where I am going."

"Won't you miss your family?"

"My family is all dead except my uncle. I will
miss him, but I am a man in my own right now. I
must make my own choices."

Jensen nodded and turned her attention back to
her surroundings as they approached the city of Sumara.

From a distance, it looked like an earthen-colored
maze with walls surrounding the closely built
houses. Every shape was angular with no softening
curves. There were no splashes of color.

Once they arrived in the city, the ancient streets
grew narrow, some of them barely wide enough for
one car. If another came toward them, Yusef would
pull as far over as he could and stop while the other
car passed.

People swathed in robes crowded the sides of the
road. Some of the women carried parcels on their
heads, moving with the sultry grace of ballerinas.
Many of the women were heavily veiled. Some of
the men and male children were in Western dress,
like Yusef. Every once in a while she'd spot a

woman or two in something similar to what she was wearing, but it occurred to her that they were probably tourists.

It just served to remind Jensen that she was a very long way from home.

"You want to shop," said Yusef, "there is great market not far. I take you."

"Thank you."

"Here comes hotel," he said proudly. "I tell you I know where it is."

On a road about twice as wide as the one they'd just left was the Metropole. There wasn't a sidewalk in front, but a dark green canopy stretched into the street. A uniformed man stepped sharply forward and opened Jensen's door, but when he tried to take her luggage from Yusef, the boy pulled it away. "No, no. I get for her."

The man raised an eyebrow, but stepped back.

Yusef carried the luggage through the large, elegant and coolly dim lobby to the front desk. A man in Western dress looked at her inquiringly.

"I have a room reserved under the name of Jensen O'Hara."

He checked his computer. "Passport and credit card, please."

Jensen lifted them from a side pocket of her purse and put them on the counter, then turned to Yusef. "How much do I owe you?"

He gave her the amount in dirim and she quickly translated it into twelve dollars.

She pulled money out of her purse. It took her a

moment to count the correct amount. Then she tried to add some for a tip.

Yusef took the fare, but shook his head at the extra. "You only pay what you owe."

"Are you sure?"

"Yes, yes. I am at your service but I don't take your money. It is my pleasure."

The clerk returned her passport and credit card. "Thank you. I have all of the other information you provided in your fax. Just sign here," he said as he placed a paper in front of her and handed her a pen.

Jensen signed and passed the paper back to him. "Are there any messages for me?"

"One moment," he said as he crossed to the other side of the counter to check his computer. "Nothing."

"Are you sure? An envelope perhaps?"

"There is nothing."

"If there is any word from a Michael Hassan, please get it to me immediately."

"Of course."

Jensen sighed. Michael should have gotten her messages by now. "Is the American Embassy far from here?"

"Not at all," said the clerk, pointing in the direction of the front doors. "Turn left as you leave the hotel. Straight down this road perhaps a thousand meters is the embassy."

"Thank you."

He handed her a room key and started to ring for someone to take her luggage, but Yusef was ahead of him, pushing aside all comers. "No, no. I take."

"I've given you room 344," said the clerk, "just as you requested in your fax."

"Thank you," Jensen said. Then she smiled at the boy. "Yusef, believe me when I say that I appreciate all you've done, but you don't have to carry my luggage. I'm sure your uncle would prefer that you spend your time driving his taxi."

Yusef shook his head and smiled at her. "No, no. I take. You come, lady."

As she followed him to the elevator, a man bumped into her, knocking her purse to the ground and spilling the contents all over the colorful carpeting.

"I'm so sorry," he said, bending down with her to help pick everything up.

"It's all right."

He handed her a fistful of things, looking into her eyes with his own velvet brown ones and touching her hand as he did so in a gesture that was strangely intimate coming, as it did, from a complete stranger.

Jensen looked at him curiously. Or was he? There was something vaguely familiar about him. "Pardon my asking, but have we met somewhere before?"

"That should be my line."

Jensen's cheeks flushed. "I didn't mean..."

He took her hand in his and helped her to her feet. "I know what you meant," he said, still holding her hand. "Are you sure you're all right? That was quite a collision."

"Yes, thank you."

He released her hand, inclined his head and walked away.

Jensen stared after him. He was dressed in a Western suit, but she guessed that he usually wore robes.

"Come on, lady," said Yusef, blocking the elevator door from closing with his narrow body.

"I'm coming. Do you know who that man is?" she asked as she stepped inside.

Yusef shrugged his shoulders as he pressed the button for her floor. "Never saw him before. Why?"

"Because I think I know him."

The doors closed and they traveled to the third floor. Taking her key, he walked quickly ahead of her so that he could have the door open when she arrived.

"Where you want Yusef to put this?" he asked as he followed her inside.

"Oh," she said as she looked around, "on the extra bed, I suppose. Thank you, Yusef."

"Is your Michael Hassan a Sumaruan?"

"Yes."

"Where does he live? Tell me and I take you there."

"I don't have an address. Just a telephone number. He went to university in America and was my brother's roommate and best friend. They've kept in touch with each other over the years. That's why I think he might be able to help me."

"You want Yusef find him for you?"

"Thank you, but no. I spoke to his houseman on the phone to tell him I was coming. He said he'd get in touch with me. I'm sure he'll be calling soon." Jensen had hoped Michael would meet her at the airport. She'd given the houseman her schedule.

"I find him anyway and make sure he call you."

Jensen smiled at him. She couldn't help herself. "Yusef, you're a very charming young man."

"Yes, yes."

"Thank you for everything. Perhaps we'll see each other again before I leave the country."

"You want anything, you ask for Yusef. Everybody know me. Everybody can find me."

Jensen looked at him curiously. "Why are you so concerned about me?"

"You nice lady. I like you, so I help."

"I appreciate that."

"So you ask for me if you need anything?"

"I will."

"Good." He flashed that wonderful grin and left, closing the door behind him.

Left alone, Jensen walked to the window and looked outside at the bustling foot traffic and backed-up automobiles.

"Oh, Henry," she whispered, "where are you?"

Chapter Two

Turning back into the room, Jensen looked around, the expression in her green eyes as lost as she felt.

This was the last place she knew for certain Henry had been and it was where her investigation had to begin. One moment he had been here, sleeping in that bed—or at least one of the beds—looking at the view from that window, walking on this floor, and the next he had disappeared into thin air.

She still didn't know whether or not he'd been kidnapped. What had that final call she'd received in Wisconsin meant? She'd waited desperately for a call back, but none had come. No one had asked for money. Only that she come here in person.

Well, she was here. The question was, what was her next move? Would that caller contact her here?

Should she strike out on her own to see what she could find?

She knew very little, despite all of her investigating before she'd come. Only that Henry had checked out of the hotel, apparently voluntarily, gotten into a long, dark limousine with someone he appeared to be on friendly terms with and vanished.

Jensen had called everyone she could think of to help her find him, but no one, not even the editor of the magazine he wrote for in New York, seemed concerned that this thirty-two-year-old man was missing.

She supposed she couldn't blame the editor. According to her, Henry was doing things like this all of the time.

Jensen tried to quell her rising panic. Henry was her only family. She adored him. He was always coming and going from her home in Wisconsin. He didn't really have a home of his own. Just a small, two-room apartment in New York that he visited a few times a year to pick up different clothes. Jensen had flown there just a day ago and searched it thoroughly without finding a single clue.

It was the farmhouse she knew he considered home—because she was there and because he had plenty of room and silence in which to roam and think and write.

What angered her most at the moment was Michael Hassan. She had called and called the man—this man who was supposedly her brother's best friend. He had called back only once while Jensen had been in New York and left a message with Mrs.

Sherman asking her to tell Jensen to stay put in Wisconsin; that he'd check into things in his country, find Henry and have him give her a call so she could stop worrying.

And that was it.

He hadn't called again.

Did he really expect her to do nothing? To sit and wait for him to decide, when it was convenient for him, to call her back about the fate of her brother?

Not a chance.

Not that she had really given him time to contact her. Jensen had flown out of New York a mere two days after that call and now she was here.

But he knew when she'd be arriving and not only hadn't he bothered to pick her up at the airport, but he hadn't even left a message for her at the front desk.

Some friend he was turning out to be.

Everyone, without exception, seemed to think she was worrying about nothing. What no one seemed to understand, though, was that if Henry had suddenly decided to follow a hot lead on a story, he would have called her. He knew she was expecting him; he knew how she worried about him; he would never have left her hanging like this. Granted, he wasn't the most reliable person in the world, but in his consideration of her, Henry was unwavering.

Almost unwavering.

There was the occasional waver. But just occasional.

This time, though, Henry hadn't called. To Jensen, that meant only one thing: he couldn't.

Her eyes filled with warm, unwanted tears. If anything had happened to him...

She dashed the backs of her hands across her eyes and instantly pulled herself together.

Michael Hassan was simply going to have to help her find Henry. That was all there was to it. And if she had to track him down and back him into a corner to get him to help, that's exactly what she'd do. Michael Hassan didn't know who he was messing with. When it came to her Henry, Jensen didn't understand the word no.

Jensen took a deep breath.

Michael Hassan. Humph.

But that man aside, there were things Jensen had to do. Like check the room.

She knelt on the floor and looked under first one bed and then the other hoping to find anything at all.

She looked behind the mirror on the dresser and ran her fingers along the back of it, looking for any kind of anomaly.

She not only opened every drawer, but pulled each one completely out and checked not only the bottoms, but the interior of the dresser itself, as well as beneath and behind it.

Crawling on her hands and knees, she went over every inch of the closet.

The same with the heavy drapes that blocked the burning rays of the sun. Every pleat, every seam, every hook was tirelessly examined.

Nothing.

Not that Jensen had seriously expected to find anything, but she had hoped.

The hotel had faxed her the list of Henry's telephone calls. There had been several to his magazine, one to her, two to Michael and several local calls, three to the same number. That was it.

Jensen looked at her watch. It was getting late and she wanted to get to the embassy before it closed for the day.

Pocketing her key, she left her room, stopping at the front desk to speak to the man who'd checked her in. "I'm going to the embassy now. In the apparently unlikely event that Mr. Michael Hassan comes while I'm out, please ask him to wait for me. It's imperative that I speak with him as soon as possible."

"Yes, Miss O'Hara."

As soon as she walked out of the air-conditioned hotel, the heat hit her with such force that it literally sucked the air from her lungs. She stopped walking for a moment. How could people live in this climate?

As soon as she had the thought, she pushed it away. They did live in it, and she was going to have to get used to it because she didn't know how long she was going to be here.

Moving through the crowds of people on the street and standing out the way only a woman in a sundress could among a population of robed and veiled citizens, Jensen walked, so wrapped up in her thoughts that she was oblivious to the stares.

And completely unaware of the ebony-skinned

man wearing indigo blue robes and headdress, following right behind her.

When Jensen walked through the wrought-iron embassy gates, the man took a position to one side, standing so erectly he appeared to be at attention.

She still didn't notice him particularly as she showed her passport to the guards at the front entrance. One of them opened the door for her and let her pass inside.

She crossed an intricately laid marble floor to the receptionist, her shoes clicking on the hard surface and echoing through the room.

"May I help you?"

"Yes. I'm Jensen O'Hara. I have an appointment to see Mr. Clayton Turner."

"I'm sorry, Miss O'Hara, but Mr. Turner has left for the weekend."

"Oh, no," said Jensen, sure that there had been some kind of misunderstanding. "That's impossible. He knew I was coming. We spoke on the telephone two days ago. He assured me he'd be here this afternoon when I arrived."

"I'm sorry, Ms. O'Hara. These things happen. He had some personal business to attend to."

Jensen agitatedly rubbed her forehead. "Is there someone else I can speak with? My brother is missing and…"

"Yes, I know," said the receptionist. "We're all concerned. Mr. Turner has full charge of the matter and he's been diligently looking into it. If you'll leave me a number where you can be reached, he'll call you on Monday morning to fill you in on any progress.''

''Monday? That's days away. Anything could have happened to Henry by Monday.''

''I'm sorry.''

''Has he told you anything? Please, if you have any information, I need to know what it is.''

The woman took pity on Jensen. ''I'm not supposed to be discussing this with you, but I really don't see what harm it will do anyone. The answer is no. We haven't been able to find a trace of your brother. But be assured that we haven't given up.''

''Just for the weekend,'' said Jensen bitterly.

''I'm sorry,'' said the woman again. ''Truly.''

Jensen sighed in resignation. It was like a conspiracy of silence that she couldn't break through. ''I'm staying at the Metropole Hotel. Mr. Turner already knows that, but remind him. And please make sure he calls me first thing Monday morning.''

''I will. You have my word.''

''Thank you.''

Jensen couldn't face going back to the hotel. What could she do there but sit in her room and worry?

So she wandered aimlessly around the city, going into shops, looking at things she had no interest in buying, still unaware of her darkly silent companion.

Ordinarily this would have been a wonderful adventure; fodder for the romance novels she so loved to write. She got out so rarely, and never to anywhere exotic like this.

But at the moment, she couldn't see beyond her worry.

Night had fallen by the time she got back to the hotel. Yusef was parked in front, leaning against his taxi. His face lit up as soon as he saw her.

"Hey, lady, you have much luck?"

"None, I'm afraid."

"Where you been?"

"The embassy."

"And no one there could help?"

"I'm afraid not."

Yusef shook his head. "I ask questions out here. Some remember your brother. He look like you, yes?"

"Yes."

"One driver remembers taking him around a lot."

Jensen was suddenly interested. "Which driver?"

"He not on duty now. Home."

"I need to speak to him."

"Yusef know where he lives. You want me to take you to him?"

"Yes, please."

"Hop in, lady."

This time, Jensen didn't hesitate as she climbed into the back and slammed the creaky door shut after her. The taxi chugged off down the road in a cloud of dark exhaust.

The man in the turban who'd been following Jensen wasted no time climbing into the driver's seat of a shiny car and taking off in pursuit. It wasn't difficult to keep them in sight. All he had to do was follow the smoke.

Yusef drove through the maze of streets using his mental map. Jensen would never have found her way there alone. When he stopped the car in front of a small home connected to seemingly dozens of other small homes that looked exactly the same, he hopped out of the car and opened the door for her.

"You stay quiet. If you must speak, whisper in my ear and I will ask questions. The man doesn't speak English anyway. And don't look directly at him. You understand?"

"Yes."

"You really should have better clothes for woman here. Tomorrow you shop."

Taking her arm, Yusef walked her to within five feet of the front door and made her stop. "You stay here." Then he moved forward and knocked on the door.

A lightly veiled woman answered and lowered her eyes as soon as she saw that it was a young man, though she couldn't help looking up through her lashes at Jensen. As soon as Yusef explained to her what he wanted, she bowed twice, backed away and closed the door.

"What's going on?" whispered Jensen.

"She is going to get her husband."

"Can't we go inside?"

"I may. You may not. Since we are together, we both stay here and he comes to us."

"All right."

A moment later, the door opened again, spilling light into the darkness. Jensen took a good look at him before lowering her eyes the way Yusef had instructed her. Yusef began asking questions in Arabic and the man answered rapid-fire.

Jensen stepped closer to Yusef and whispered in his ear. "What's he saying?"

"He says he took your brother many places."

"What places?"

Yusef asked.

"Well?" asked Jensen.

"Two private homes and three businesses."

"Did any of those private homes belong to Michael Hassan?" asked Jensen.

Yusef asked the question and listened to the answer. "He doesn't know," said Yusef. "All he knows are addresses."

"Get them."

"Yes, yes, of course."

"Did my brother say anything to him?"

Again, Yusef asked the question and waited for the answer. "Not directly," said Yusef. "But he overheard your brother say to another man that he had one more bit of research to do and was looking forward to going home after that."

"When did he hear this conversation?"

Yusef asked. "A week ago Sunday. He remembers because it was same day of his daughter's birth."

"Did he see my brother at all after that?"

Yusef asked. "Only one time, when he left hotel with his backpack and entered a fancy car driven by a man in a suit. That was last he saw of your brother."

"Thank him for me, please," said Jensen, "and

give him this.'' She reached into her purse and took out a handful of coins, which she instinctively knew to give to Yusef for transfer to the man.

The man bowed several times and watched while Yusef walked Jensen back to his taxi.

"We go now to the places your brother went, yes?"

"Yes, please."

At the first private house, Jensen was surprised by its elegance. It was large and well maintained, even though it still blended in with those surrounding it. There was even a gate to keep out strangers, with a buzzer on an outside pillar. No one answered their call.

The second private home was just as large. When Yusef answered the voice that came over the speaker, explaining who Jensen was and that she wished to speak with them, the voice that replied was hostile and cut them off.

"I wonder what my brother could possibly have done to have provoked that kind of reaction?" she wondered aloud.

"I don't know, but you must not come back here alone."

"I wouldn't even know how to begin to find it. All the streets and homes look the same to me."

Yusef nodded. "That's why Yusef is the taxi driver and you are the passenger."

Jensen smiled.

Yusef saw it in the rearview mirror. "You pretty when you smile. Should do it more often."

"I will when I find my brother."

"I understand. We go to businesses now." Yusef aimed the taxi in what Jensen believed to be the general direction of the hotel, but turned off onto some side streets before they got there.

Seedy side streets.

Every city in the world had them, apparently.

As Yusef parked the taxi, he turned to Jensen. "You stay here and keep doors locked. I go inside and ask about your brother."

Jensen touched his shoulder. "I should go with you."

"No place for lady, believe me. I know."

Jensen looked at the bearded men loitering in front of the place, staring at the taxi.

Staring at her.

"Then it's no place for a child."

That was completely the wrong thing to say to him. "Yusef is no child! Now stay here and lock doors."

He got out and slammed the door with a bit more force than necessary, still furious with her assessment of his age. Jensen quickly reached around and punched down all of the locks.

Even though she avoided looking at the men, she could feel their eyes on her. She sank lower into her seat.

It didn't help. They began to surround the taxi, like crows readying for a feast.

Then there was a shout; a deep throated shout that certainly hadn't come from little Yusef.

Jensen looked up and saw a huge man in indigo

blue robes and a turban, his hand resting on the butt of his sheathed sword, as he faced the men down.

The man didn't utter another word as he stood near the rear window of the taxi, apparently ready to do battle on her behalf. He didn't have to speak. The men backed away and averted their eyes from Jensen.

Yusef came out of the little building at that moment and looked with huge eyes at the man in blue. The man spoke only a few words. Yusef nodded his head and hurried to the car. When he pulled on the door handle, it was locked.

Jensen quickly reached out and pulled the pin up.

Yusef scooted behind the wheel, fired up the engine and laid rubber as he peeled out of there.

"Who was that man?" asked Jensen.

"What man?"

"Don't be obtuse," she scolded. "The one in the blue."

"Just a man. We go back to hotel now."

"What about the other businesses?"

"No more tonight. Maybe tomorrow."

She put her hand on his shoulder. "Did something happen inside there?" she asked.

"No. Yusef just a little scared."

Jensen nodded. "Me, too. I guess you're right. We've had enough for one night."

"We go other places in daylight."

"All right." She sat back in her seat. "Yusef?"

"Yes, lady?"

"Thank you for everything you've done."

He smiled in the rearview mirror. "No problem."

As he parked in front of the hotel, Yusef hopped out and opened the door for her.

"How much?"

He suddenly looked down. "I didn't keep track of the meter."

Jensen pressed the equivalent of a hundred dollars into his hand and folded his fingers around it. "This is for everything you've done. Please don't turn it down. I'll be insulted if you do."

He couldn't see what she'd given him, but he knew it was a lot. "Okay, lady. But we go searching again tomorrow."

"Thank you, Yusef." She couldn't help herself as she leaned forward and kissed his forehead.

He flushed straight to the roots of his hair.

"You'll find that we Americans are incorrigibly affectionate," she said with a smile as she walked into the hotel.

She went straight to the desk. The same man was there. Before she could say a word, he shook his head. "I'm sorry, Miss O'Hara, but Mr. Hassan did not call. You have no messages."

"Thank you."

Looking around, she saw a sign with an arrow pointing the way to the hotel restaurant. Jensen felt less conspicuous among other tourists and businessmen and decided to eat there.

Sitting at a table alone, she ordered couscous—one of the few familiar things on the menu—along with a bottle of mineral water. When the food came, she spent more time pushing it around her plate than actually eating it. Worry about her brother and the heat had sapped what little appetite she had.

She signed the bill and then headed for her room.

As she got off the elevator and began to walk down the hall, she saw a dark-skinned man at the far end dressed in indigo robes. He stood with his legs apart, arms folded across his chest. It might have been the same man who'd stood off those men earlier, but she hadn't seen his face. Besides, what would he be doing here?

Jensen smiled at him, but there was no response.

Surprise. No one except Yusef had smiled at her all day. It definitely wasn't the same man.

Unlocking her door, she stepped into her dark room and closed the door behind her before turning on the light. As soon as it snapped on, she was grabbed from behind. A scream tore into her throat, but before she could make any noise, a hand was clamped over her mouth.

As she struggled against the man's hold on her, Jensen bit his hand, just the way she'd been taught in a self-defense class. He swore, but didn't remove his hand.

Then she tried to elbow him in the groin, but he blocked her and got her in a shoulder lock that immobilized her from the waist up. Even as he lifted her off the floor, she kicked out. Their furious dance took them across the room until they both lost their balance and landed in a tangled body heap on the bed.

Jensen, squirming frantically, was pinned beneath the heavy body of the robed man. His hand still

BRITTANY YOUNG 39

covered her mouth, but he'd learned his lesson. There was no way for her to bite him again.

He wrapped himself around her so tightly that she couldn't move. How was it possible for anyone to be that strong?

"Stop struggling," ordered the man in perfect English.

She had no choice. She couldn't have moved if she'd wanted to.

"I haven't come to hurt you. I only want to talk. If I uncover your mouth will you promise not to scream?"

Jensen thought about it for a moment.

"Give me your word."

She nodded—reluctantly.

He tentatively uncovered her mouth, but kept his hand at the ready in case it was needed.

Jensen's whole body was tense, ready to spring at the slightest physical give on his part.

There was none. None at all. The man seemed to know what she was thinking and held her as tightly as ever.

Her breathing was ragged and gasping from the fight as she looked at the man who had attacked her. The man who could still hurt her if he chose.

His bronze face was directly above hers, inches away. She could feel his breath on her skin, nearly as ragged as hers.

She could feel the steady, hard hammering of his heart, pressed against her breasts.

And he was looking at her with a pair of the bluest eyes she'd ever seen.

Chapter Three

"I'm Michael Hassan," he said. "Please relax. You have no reason to fear me."

"Michael Hassan?" she asked. "You're Michael Hassan?" Her voice was suddenly angry. "How dare you attack me like this. Get off of me this instant!"

With a hand on either side of her, he pushed himself away into a standing position.

"I would hardly call it an attack," he said as he walked into the bathroom to hold his injured hand under cold running water. "I was trying to keep you from screaming."

The door suddenly crashed open and the man in the blue robes stood there, every muscle at attention, his sword drawn, his furious eyes on Jensen.

Jensen was so stunned she couldn't have

screamed if she'd wanted to. She just lay there and waited to be run through. All she could think of was that this was such an odd way to die in this day and age. Too bad she wouldn't live to put it in one of her books.

Michael Hassan turned off the water and walked back into the room. He said something in Arabic and the man sheathed his sword, bowed his head and backed out of the room. He couldn't close the door, of course, because it was broken.

Jensen put her hand over her heart and closed her eyes as she lay back on the bed.

"Are you all right?" asked Michael.

"Any more surprises?"

A corner of his mouth lifted. "I think you've had enough for one evening."

She rose from the bed with as much dignity as she could muster and brushed down her crumpled dress. "Would you mind telling me what's going on? Who was that man?"

"That's Ali. He works for me. I guess you could say he's my bodyguard."

"And why do you need a bodyguard? To save you from the women whose rooms you sneak into?"

He held up his hand, which clearly showed her teeth marks. "I'm thinking about adding that to his list of duties."

Jensen hated to hurt anyone, whatever the circumstances. She walked over to him and took his hand in hers to examine the damage. "You should get that looked at by a doctor so it doesn't get infected. Bites aren't anything to mess with."

Michael's eyes moved slowly over her delicate profile and that long, beautiful hair. "You look like a feminine version of Henry. I would have known you anywhere."

Jensen's eyes met his. She was suddenly self-conscious about touching him and released his hand. "When was the last time you heard from my brother?"

"Around the same time you did. He called to say he was coming to see me, but didn't show up."

"And that didn't worry you?"

"Not really. He's done that before. Many times. He also said he was following a hot story that could be one of the biggest of his career. I assumed then—and assume now—that he's following that story, whatever it is."

"He would have called me."

"This isn't America, Jensen. There aren't phones around every corner."

"Henry would have found a way. He knew I was expecting him. He never, ever just disappears."

"I can see you don't know your brother nearly as well as you think you do."

Jensen wanted to tell him to take his injured hand and his bodyguard and, well, go away, to put it politely. But this was about Henry, not her. She took a deep breath and mentally counted to ten. "I need your help to find him."

"What if he doesn't want to be found?"

"Then he can tell me to go away. But in order for him to do that, I have to find him first."

Michael looked at her for a long moment. "No."

Jensen blinked. "That's your answer? Your best friend is missing and that's it? Just 'no'?"

"That's it."

"First you terrorize me and then that...that...Ali person out there breaks in my door and nearly runs me through with a sword and you aren't even going to help me?"

"When Henry wants to be found, he'll surface. In the meantime, you should turn around and go back to America."

Jensen walked to the empty doorway and pointed into the hall. "Get out."

Michael walked up to her, put a finger under her chin and raised her face so she had no choice but to look at him. "Go home, Jensen O'Hara. This is no place for a woman alone. Henry would be the first one to tell you that."

She slapped his hand away. "I can't believe you're my brother's best friend. You're nothing like him. And you, of all people, should be as concerned as I am."

"Go home," he repeated. "You'll accomplish nothing here but to get into trouble. If it hadn't been for Ali tonight, who knows what might have happened in the street."

"So that was him." She frowned. "What was your bodyguard doing following me?"

"I sent him to keep a careful eye on you. You seemed to me somehow destined for trouble."

She couldn't bring herself to thank him. "Well, what I do from this moment forward is none of your business. Now leave my room before I call the police."

Michael inclined his head. "As you wish."

And as quickly as that, he and his bodyguard were gone. Vanished. The only evidence that they'd ever been there was the broken door.

Jensen walked to the telephone and calmly dialed the front desk. "I need a new room," she said when a man answered. "Someone's broken my door down."

Jensen went downstairs to the restaurant for breakfast the next morning. The sundress was replaced with loose jeans and a white blouse tucked in at the waist. The more skin she covered up, the better. She should have realized that yesterday.

A waiter approached her table with a portable telephone. "Excuse me," he said, "but you have a phone call."

"Are you sure it's for me?"

"Yes, ma'am."

Jensen took the phone. "Hello?"

"Miss O'Hara?"

"Yes."

"This is Clayton Turner from the embassy."

"Oh, hello! I understood from the receptionist that you weren't coming back until Monday."

"There was an emergency at the office. Anyway, the good news is that I have some information for you about your brother. I wanted to share it with you as soon as possible."

Jensen sat up straight. "Thank you so much! I'm listening."

"It's my understanding from a reliable source who wishes to remain anonymous that your brother ventured into the desert, headed for a small town called Adjani, last week after a news story."

"Is he all right?"

"That's not known at this time. I believe he was in good health the last time our source saw him, but was in the company of some dangerous individuals."

"Is there some way I can get to my brother? A bus? A train? Any way at all?"

"I took the liberty of arranging for a guide to meet with you in the hotel lobby in exactly one hour. Be packed and ready to leave at that time. Don't be late."

"I'll be ready. Thank you!" said Jensen.

"Not at all."

"I appreciate your taking me seriously."

"Good luck with your search. I hope you call me when you return to let me know how things turn out."

"I will. Goodbye."

"Goodbye, Miss O'Hara."

Jensen set the phone on the table and looked at her watch. It was ten o'clock.

After quickly signing for her breakfast, Jensen went to her room, packed and rolled her suitcase into the lobby. "I'd like to check out," she told the clerk.

He punched up her information on the computer and readied her bill within minutes.

"May I leave my suitcase with you behind the desk until my guide arrives?"

"Of course." He signaled a man in uniform to take the suitcase, then handed her a bill and a pen.

Jensen looked it over and signed it. "Thank you."

"Lady! Lady!"

She would have known that voice anywhere. Turning, she smiled at the young man walking quickly toward her. "Yusef. Are you driving again today?"

"Not today. My uncle is on duty. I come see you. Maybe go to other businesses. Any luckiness finding your brother?"

"Yes. Very good luckiness, as a matter of fact. I just got a call from Mr. Turner who's with the American embassy. He managed to find out where my brother was last seen and is sending a guide to escort me into the desert."

"You go into desert?"

"Yes."

Yusef shook his head. "Not good. Not good. Desert a very dangerous place. No place for woman."

"I'm beginning to think that no place around here is safe for a woman. Including her own room."

"This not funny."

Jensen smiled at him. She couldn't help it. "Thanks for worrying, but there's no need. If Mr. Turner is sending a guide, he must be a good one. I'm sure no one from the embassy would knowingly send an American citizen into danger."

"I still don't like. Desert very big place. Bigger than all of United States. Easy to get lost. Sheik would not approve."

Jensen looked at him curiously. "The sheik wouldn't approve?" she asked. "What difference could what I do make to the sheik?"

"Sheik is your friend."

"Who told you that? I've never met the man."

"He came to your room last night."

Jensen suddenly understood. "Oh, no, no. That was my brother's friend, Michael Hassan."

Yusef nodded. "Yes." And he proceeded to rattle off a ten part list of names that ended with Michael Hassan. "His mother, as I told you, was American, so she call him Michael. When you spoke of him yesterday, I didn't realize they were the same man. Then I see him last night and I know."

Jensen was having trouble taking this in. "You're saying that Michael Hassan, the man I met with last night—my brother's best friend—is the sheik—the king of Sumaru?"

"Yes, yes. Now you are understanding me. He pay you very great honor by visiting you here last night."

"That depends on your perspective," she said dryly.

"It not look too good to others, though, so I not say anything." He made a zipping motion across his mouth with his fingers.

"You mean because he was in my room?"

"Yes, yes. That look very bad. Very, very bad."

As they spoke, a man walked in, fully robed as

were most of the men she'd seen, his head covered in the traditional flowing white cloth with the band around the top to hold it in place. He walked straight to her. "Ms. O'Hara?" he asked in a thick accent.

"Yes." She extended her hand, which he ignored.

He handed her a note. "This is your guide. He speaks almost no English, so communication between you will be all but impossible, but he is very capable and knows the desert well. He knows where your brother was last and will take you there. Your journey should take approximately three days. Yours in service, Clayton Turner."

Yusef took the note from Jensen when she was finished and read it himself.

"My luggage is over there," she said, pointing to the front desk.

The man looked blankly at her.

"My luggage. There."

Another blank look.

Raising her hand to indicate "never mind," she went to the desk and got the suitcase herself while shouldering her backpack.

The man took the suitcase from her and carried it outside to his waiting very old, very beat-up four-wheel drive and put it into the back along with a lot of other gear already stowed there.

He pointed at the passenger door, which Jensen took as a sign that she was to get into the car.

Yusef ran up to her and placed his body between Jensen and the door. "I still don't think you should go with this man. You need to talk to sheik first."

"He has nothing to do with this, Yusef. He refused to help me look for my brother."

"He not like you going into desert with stranger, embassy or no embassy. I know this."

Jensen impulsively kissed him on the forehead just as she had last night. "Thank you for caring, Yusef. If it were in my power to choose a little brother, you'd be the one. But I'm going. I have to. If it were your brother who was missing, wouldn't you go?"

Yusef, still blushing from the kiss, frowned. "Yes, yes. I suppose. But I not woman."

"Yusef..."

It was with great and obvious reluctance that he opened the car door for her.

Jensen climbed inside and Yusef closed the door.

The guide turned the key in the ignition. It seemed to take a great deal of effort on the part of the engine to start, but it finally did. Without waiting to make sure that Yusef was clear, he gunned the accelerator and pulled into traffic.

Jensen turned in her seat and waved to Yusef, who looked like a forlorn little boy standing in the middle of the road, then turned back to face forward.

She looked for a seat belt but there wasn't one.

Then she glanced at the stone-faced man beside her.

With a great internal sigh, Jensen readied herself for a *loooong* three days.

As they left the city, traffic gradually grew more sparse. Squared off settlements of homes grew fewer and farther between. Where once one could see small blocks of sand here and there, now it began to take over the vista to the exclusion of nearly everything else.

After an hour, they left the main highway and took a two-lane offshoot that looked like a road to nowhere. It went straight into the desert and desert was all Jensen could see. Ripples of sand; waves created by wind; dunes that seemed to go on for miles.

The faded road itself seemed to disappear into the sand.

And the heat. Unbelievable. The relentless sun was directly overhead, pounding the roof of the car. Needless to say, there was no air conditioning. Jensen left her window open just for the wind, but the problem with that was the sand. After a while it clung to her perspiration-sticky skin. She ran her fingers across her forehead and could feel the scratchy residue.

Reaching into her purse, Jensen pulled out her sunglasses and slipped them onto her nose. Normally her eyes weren't terribly sun sensitive, but this was a completely different kind of light than she was used to. This gave her a headache.

When they'd first started down the road, there had actually been some scattered traffic. When they'd been driving for several hours, that traffic had trickled into practically nothing.

They came to a one-pump service station. A man in robes walked out of a little house and spoke with the guide.

Jensen climbed out of the car and stretched before

going to the rear of the car and searching through the gear for some water. She found a bottle and showed it to the guide.

He brusquely nodded his head to affirm that it was okay for her to drink.

She pulled up the stopper and squirted some into her mouth. It was hot, like the air, but at least it was liquid and rinsed the sand from her mouth.

At a signal from the guide, she climbed back into the car, taking the water with her.

Half an hour later, the guide took the car off the road completely and headed directly into the desert. Plumes of choking sand rose behind them.

They drove for another five hours, during which Jensen saw one of the most remarkable sunsets of her life. The guide stopped when it grew dark and motioned to her to sleep in the back seat. He pulled bedding out of the back of the car and handed it to her, then pulled some out for himself and signaled to her that he would be sleeping elsewhere.

The heat had sapped her energy and her appetite. She didn't even bother to ask him about dinner. Not that he would have understood her anyway.

Even now, it was still hot from the warmth rising from the sand. There was no escaping it.

Jensen spread a sleeping bag onto the back seat and lay on top of it, her arm across her forehead.

What if Henry wasn't there when she got to wherever she was going? What would she do then?

She was too tired to think about it.

Everything went black. Jensen fell into an absolutely sound sleep that lasted uninterrupted all night long.

It was the heat that awakened her. It began filling the car even before the sun had completely risen.

Jensen watched it through squinted eyes for several minutes before stiffly rising from the back seat and stepping out onto the sand. She reached back inside for her bottle of water and squirted some into her mouth, rinsed it around and spit it out.

Pushing the stopper back in, she set the bottle back inside the car and looked around for the guide.

There was no sign of him.

"Hello!" she called out.

No answer.

"Hello!" she yelled louder.

Nothing.

Jensen walked all the way around the car looking for some sign of the man. It wasn't as though there was anything for him to hide behind. He was, quite simply, gone without a trace.

Jensen couldn't believe it! He'd just left her there, in the middle of nowhere, surrounded by sand with no landmarks in sight. She had no idea where she was, where they were going or how to get back.

She furiously slammed her foot into the side of the car. "Damn you!" she screamed. "Where are you?"

There wasn't even an echo. It was as though she hadn't made a sound.

God, the heat.

Okay. She had to think.

Her mind ran in thirty directions at once.

Calm down.

Focus.

Focus. "Come on, Jensen," she said aloud. "Come on."

She looked at the car. The car was the key to her rescue. If she could turn the car around and follow the tracks made the day before, she'd find her way back.

This was good. This was a plan.

She walked around to the back of the car. Yes. There were the tracks. This could work.

Jensen climbed into the car. The keys were in the ignition. She turned them.

Nothing.

She turned them again.

Nothing! Not a chug or a pop or a grind. Absolutely nothing.

Jensen walked around to the hood. It was slightly open. She raised it the rest of the way and looked at what to her was completely foreign territory except for the battery—which wasn't where it should have been. In fact, it wasn't there at all.

Great.

And even Jensen knew that the fistful of broken wires hanging out of a black cable shouldn't have looked that way.

"Don't panic," she whispered. "Everything will be fine."

But she couldn't help the fear that was rising like bile in her throat. She was terrified.

What next?

Water. She had to have water to survive. She'd never even make it through the day without it.

Walking around to the back of the car, she opened the liftgate, climbed inside and searched through the things, tossing them out onto the sand when she'd finished searching them. There was a red tent and her suitcase, of course. Her backpack. An empty gasoline can.

No water.

Jensen leaned over the back seat and picked up the water bottle she had so carelessly tossed inside earlier, hugging it to her. There were perhaps four swallows left.

The inside of the still car was like an oven. Outside wasn't much better. It had to be 120 degrees.

She needed shade. The car provided some, but the heat coming off the metal was more than she could bear.

Climbing out of the rear, she emptied the nylon bag containing the tent.

There were no directions, of course, and she'd never set one up before. Her idea of roughing it up to this point was a weekend at the Holiday Inn.

Piece by piece, she set everything out on the sand and tried to figure out what made sense. It took her an hour to get something up, but it was more like a lean-to than a tent.

Fine. It was still shade.

Laying a blanket on the ground beneath it, Jensen took her water and sat down. She allowed herself a small sip.

Jensen finally had to admit to herself that she

didn't have a clue what to do to get herself out of this mess. It wouldn't do her any good to follow the car tracks on foot because they'd traveled for hours yesterday without seeing a single living creature.

She'd never be able to make it back to the road. It had to be nearly 150 miles away.

She was afraid to go forward because she didn't know what was there. Yusef's words about the size of the Sahara rang in her ears: Larger than the United States.

Jensen lifted a handful of sun-bleached grains and let them sift slowly through her fingers. No one knew where she was except the guide, and he certainly wasn't going to come back for her.

Was this what had happened to Henry? Her dear Henry? Had someone just dumped him in the desert? Was he now part of the sand, the way she was going to be before very long?

With her legs crossed in front of her, Jensen went through her suitcase to see if there was anything useful. She pulled out a few things to use for bedding later.

In her backpack she found some peanuts she'd saved from the plane and an oatmeal cookie she carefully wrapped in tissues.

The peanuts were salty, so she decided against them. They'd only make her thirstier. Though she seemed to remember reading somewhere that one should have salt at times like this.

It didn't matter.

But she could nibble the cookie when she was

hungry. If done carefully, it would last her for two days.

One cookie for two days. And she was already starving from no dinner the night before.

She took a small bite, carefully rewrapped it and put it back in the sack.

Then she took out her journal, which she carried everywhere, and a pen, and began to write. Not particularly because she had anything she wanted to say, but because she needed to pass the time and forget about the heat.

God, the heat.

The unbearable, suffocating heat.

She closed her eyes and thought of Wisconsin with all of its grass and fields, forests and lakes.

Her cool little farm with all the paths through the forest.

Her favorite path, where sunlight poured through the leaves making patterns on the ground.

As night fell, she took another bite of her cookie, a small sip of water and watched her first real desert sunset, her arms wrapped around her legs, her chin on her knees.

Spectacular wasn't a strong enough word. Extraordinary. Colors more vivid than any she'd ever seen.

She watched as it peaked and then dimmed into night.

Suddenly she realized that the heat had faded. In fact, it was almost cool. Not by Wisconsin standards, of course, but by Sahara standards it was really pleasant.

Jensen lay on her makeshift bed and rested her head on her backpack. Hunger gnawed at her. Thirst made swallowing difficult. But she'd made it through the day.

If this were one of her novels, her hero would come riding to her rescue, sweep her up in his arms and carry her away.

She smiled.

Maybe tomorrow.

Then it was time to sleep.

Chapter Four

A roar thundered overhead and the earth beneath her shook.

Jensen, her heart racing, her hands over her ears, shot straight up from a sound sleep.

Looking out from under her little lean-to, she saw military jets flying low over the sand.

Maneuvers, no doubt.

She didn't even bother to leave the shade of the tent to wave at them. At the speed they were going, they'd never see her anyway. And what if they did? She was just some desert creature. How could they possibly know she needed help?

As she watched, the jets turned in the distance and came back to buzz her again.

She'd always loved military jets with their power

and precision. There was something very sensuous about the vibration they left behind. She felt it now.

And then there was silence.

Another day.

Jensen rationed herself down to just coating her tongue with water. She spent the day beneath her shelter, conserving her energy and her need for water.

But she was so thirsty. So incredibly thirsty. Her lips were dry and beginning to crack.

Her lips!

Reaching into her backpack, she pulled out her lip moisturizer and liberally smeared it on. It helped.

Strange. Jensen wasn't a hopeless kind of person. On the contrary, she was usually very upbeat about things. But, in this situation, logic defied any hopeful attitude she attempted.

Logic told Jensen that she was going to die. She knew with complete certainty that if no one found her in the next eighteen hours, it would be too late.

And she found she was amazingly accepting of it.

Pulling out her journal, she began to write about what she was feeling; regrets about things done and undone.

Then she set it aside and watched from the safety of her shelter as the sun passed its peak in the sky and started down.

That's when she felt it.

Another vibration.

Not like the jets, though. This one was barely noticeable at first, but grew stronger and louder as the minutes passed.

An earthquake?

Jensen rose slowly to her feet and looked in the direction of the noise. At first, all she could see were clouds of dust rising in the hot air.

A sandstorm?

But then she saw the horsemen, their desert robes flowing, riding straight toward her. She counted four of them. Maybe more. It was difficult to see.

Help at last!

Moving away from the tent, she ran toward the riders, waving her arms at them. They were within a hundred yards when she suddenly sensed something behind her and turned to find a horseman just feet away. Before she could react, he leaned toward her, grabbing her around the waist and hoisting her onto his horse in front of him.

"What are you...." she began. "Put me down!"

The man pulled sharply on the horse's reins to stop it in midgallop. The horse automatically reared, slamming Jensen's back into the man's strong chest.

"I said put me down!" she demanded as the horse danced restlessly beneath them.

"Don't speak," said the man against her ear.

Jensen turned her head and found herself looking into a pair of familiar blue eyes. "You again!" she said furiously. "Always attacking me from behind. What's wrong with you?"

"If you value your life," said Michael, "and mine—you will be silent until those men leave."

She looked over Michael's shoulder and saw the indigo-robed bodyguard seated on a horse just a few feet away with a camel in tow. "You're a psychopath. A card-carrying psychopath. I don't have time for this nonsense. You said you didn't want to help and I took you at your word. Well, I don't need you to rescue me, either. Now, let me off this horse or so help me I'll bite your other hand."

"Silence!" hissed Michael as he stared straight ahead. "Not another word."

It was the way he said it. Jensen stopped arguing and turned to face the approaching strangers. She'd been so overjoyed just to see another person that she hadn't noticed anything else about them.

Now she realized there was an ominous quality in their movement; their bearing. Something she hadn't sensed in her rush for rescue.

One man stopped his horse ahead of the others, perhaps ten feet away. He spoke in Arabic.

Michael's arm tightened protectively around Jensen's waist as he responded with one word.

The other man's eyes moved over her body with deliberate and rude slowness, tracing every curve and making it abundantly clear to Jensen what her fate would have been with him.

She pressed her body closer to Michael's.

As the other man rode closer, bringing his horse up next to theirs, Michael placed his mouth near her ear. "Don't move, Jensen," he whispered. "Whatever happens, don't move. Don't speak."

Jensen sat rigidly as the man on the other horse reached out and touched her hair. He stroked it for a moment, then lifted her ponytail and let the strands run through his fingers. He seemed to come to some kind of decision and spoke again.

As before, Michael answered with one word.

The other one's eyes narrowed on her for a long time, no doubt pondering his next move.

Ali moved closer. His hand was on the hilt of his sword.

The other man saw this.

Without saying anything else, he turned his horse and rode away with the others following him.

Jensen was more shaken than she cared to admit. "What was that all about?"

Michael climbed down from the horse then put his hands at her waist as he lifted her to the ground, leaving them there as he looked into her eyes. "He wanted to buy you from me."

Jensen looked back at him in disbelief. "You're not serious. You can't be."

"If he'd gotten to you first, I would have had to buy you from him. Although judging from the way he was looking at you, I don't think he would have sold you to me." A corner of his mouth lifted. "At least not right away…"

Jensen stared at him without smiling. "You think this is funny? You people are all nuts."

"Actually, it's not funny at all," said Michael. "There's quite a lively white slavery trade in this part of the world. A woman who looks like you with your blond hair and green eyes and, frankly, your figure, would bring top dollar."

Jensen shivered with repugnance. "How did you know I was out here?"

"A young man by the name of Yusef tracked me down. He was concerned and thought I should be as well. Would you care to tell me what's going on?''

"I got a call from Clayton Turner at the American Embassy yesterday morning telling me he had word of my brother and was sending a guide to take me to the last place Henry was seen. This man showed up at the hotel, handed me a note from Turner, drove me out here and when I awoke this morning, he was gone.''

"Would this be the note?'' he asked, handing her a familiar slip of paper.

Jensen glanced at it. "Yes. But how did you…''

"Yusef,'' they both said at the same time.

Jensen shook her head. "I don't understand what's going on. Why would someone from the embassy send me out here with a guide like that? It doesn't make any sense.''

"I spoke with Clayton Turner yesterday,'' said Michael, "and he told me he never called you and never sent a guide.''

"If he didn't,'' said Jensen with a frown, "who did?''

"Clearly someone who wants you out of the way.''

"Because of Henry?''

"I'd say that's a reasonable conclusion.''

"But why?''

"That's what we have to find out.''

Jensen looked at Michael for a long moment. "Are you saying you're going to help me?''

"Do I have a choice?''

"You certainly do. You could just walk away and leave me here to die."

"The thought crossed my mind," he said evenly.

"I'm sure it did. You could also take me back to the city and leave me there."

"That thought also crossed my mind."

Jensen tilted her head to one side. "But you aren't going to do either of those things, are you? Why not?"

"Henry is my good friend. You're his family. He would want me to see to your safety. And clearly someone wants you out of the way badly enough to leave you in the middle of the desert with no provisions. Besides which, I think you're right. Something is fishy about the way Henry disappeared. It was a little too sudden, even for Henry."

"I've already told you that Henry is completely reliable," said Jensen defensively.

"In your world, the world of family, that may well be. He is a man who keeps his promises. But in the world of our friendship, he's been known to chase a woman or two, not to mention potential story leads, and not keep to any schedule. That's why I wasn't overly concerned when you called."

"But you are now?"

"He's been gone too long. Even if you had left when I asked you, I would have undertaken my own investigation."

Jensen, with her sunburned cheeks and bright green eyes, smiled at Michael.

She took his breath away. He couldn't afford to let any woman make him feel that way, much less some American romance novelist. He went immediately on the defensive and withdrew from her.

"And now," she said, "may I please have some water?"

Michael signaled his bodyguard who instantly handed him a bottle of water. Michael opened it and handed it to her. "Just drink in little sips for now."

Jensen did as he suggested. "It's difficult. I want to chug the entire bottle."

"I know, but take your time."

"I don't know what I would have done if you hadn't come after me." Even as she warmed toward her brother's friend, Jensen felt Michael withdraw.

Her smile faded. "Do you have any leads?"

"Yes. I discovered that Henry apparently overheard a conversation about a white slave auction in a desert village called Adjani that was coming up in a few days and decided to wangle himself an invitation so he could write a story about it."

"And?"

"He made arrangements for a trek across the desert to get to Adjani and that's the last anyone saw of him."

"So I was right in my thinking last night. He could have ended up stranded out here the way I just did?"

"That's one possibility. Or he could already have reached Adjani safely."

"What do we do?"

"I've sent search planes out over the desert. Naturally it's impossible for them to search the whole area, but they can cover a lot of ground. That's how

I—'' he hesitated over his next words ''—found you.''

''I'm surprised you didn't swoop down in a helicopter to rescue me.''

A corner of his mouth lifted. ''I thought horses more in keeping with your romantic novels.''

A dimple flashed in her cheek. ''What about a car?''

''Still not up to your standards.'' He almost smiled. ''The truth is that where we're going from here, cars can't travel. And I didn't want to bring the military into this in any obvious way, which a helicopter would have done.''

''What about the jets?''

''Military maneuvers, plain and simple. No cause for concern by neighboring countries.''

''You put a lot of thought into this rescue.''

''One must if one is to avoid war.'' He looked at her for a long moment. ''I suppose it's pointless of me to ask you to go home and wait for word.''

''Pointless,'' she agreed.

''I thought as much. It would appear, then, that you and I will be going to Adjani together.'' He inclined his head toward the car. ''Take what you need for tonight and tomorrow. I'll send someone for the rest of your things.''

Jensen leaned into her tent and pulled clean clothes out of her suitcase, her toiletries and her journal and stuffed them into her backpack. She went back to the car and searched for her purse, but it was gone, along with her money and passport. No doubt taken by the guide.

"Ready?" asked Michael.

She took a last look around. "Yes."

Michael gave her a hand up onto the horse, then swung himself up behind her as he shouted something to Ali.

The bodyguard inclined his head and rode about twenty feet in front and to one side so that the sand churned up by his horse's hooves and those of the camel didn't fly up at them.

The pace was slow, the horses moving in rhythm with the camel. Jensen relaxed after a few minutes and allowed herself to lean her back against Michael's chest. His arms tightened on either side of her as he held the reins.

Michael was exactly right. Everything that was happening was like a scene from one of her novels. Woman lost in desert, rescued by the handsome sheik and riding on horseback to...

She turned her head slightly. "Where are we going?"

"To one of my homes."

...one of his homes, finished Jensen in her mind.

"But we'll have to break our journey at one of my permanent camps this evening before continuing on."

"Why can't we just go straight to Adjani?"

"It's difficult to reach. There's an airport, but it belongs to another sheik. The only other access is one very bad road. That's why the slave traders use it for their auctions. Strangers are noticed and it's impossible to stage a raid without warning the entire city that it's coming. We'll have to blend in as best we can. That means you have to completely change your appearance."

"Is that why we're stopping at your home?"

"Yes. My sister will help you with your mannerisms and your clothing."

"My mannerisms?"

She didn't see Michael smile, but she sensed it. "You carry yourself in far too bold a fashion. You need to walk with smaller steps with your head slightly bowed, eyes lowered. You must never look at men directly. You must never speak to them unless spoken to first."

"Anything else?"

"You must keep your body, your face and your hair covered at all times." He moved his mouth closer to her ear, and Jensen felt an unaccustomed jolt through her body at the contact. "As you are now, you dangerously stand out. If you insist on going, you have to look like everyone else. You must not—cannot—draw attention to yourself. Do you understand this?"

"Yes."

"I mean it, Jensen. From here on, we do things my way. This is my part of the world, not yours. If you can't do as you're told, you'll be putting both us and your brother at risk."

"I understand. Really. I just feel helpless. Like Henry needs me and I'm wasting time."

"I've already sent a man ahead of us to discreetly find out what he can."

"Thank you."

Silence fell between them.

They rode in the heat for more than two hours with stops for water carried by Ali for the animals and themselves. By the time Jensen spotted the tent, a splash of blue against the monochromatic beige of the sand, she was drenched in perspiration.

"What I wouldn't give for a long, cool shower," she said as she slid from the horse.

"I'm afraid you'll have to settle for a sponge bath."

"I know. It was just a wish."

"And you might as well wait until it's time to sleep. It's nearing sunset now. We'll go to bed soon thereafter and get an early start to my home in the morning."

Ali took the horses to a canvas lean-to where there was food and water.

Jensen watched as he walked away from them. "He's a frightening man."

"Yes," said Michael, "he is."

"Would he really have killed me in that hotel room if he'd thought I were there to harm you?"

"Without blinking an eye. Just as he'll now kill to protect you because you're a friend of mine."

"Even though he doesn't like me?"

"What makes you think that?"

"The way he looks at me."

"He looks at everyone the same way."

"That's comforting."

The corners of Michael's mouth hinted at a smile. "Make yourself at ease here. Have something cool to drink. We'll eat soon."

"Thank you."

He walked away from her, from the small encampment, across the ripples of undisturbed sand, up a dune and stood looking out at the desert, his hands clasped behind his back.

Ali, apparently finished with the horses, walked past her and ducked through the doorway of the tent.

Jensen didn't know what to do with herself. She wasn't about to go inside the tent, curious though she was.

Rather than remain where she was, she followed Michael up the dune. The walk turned out to be harder than it looked. The sand shifted beneath her feet and there were times when she lost three steps for every one she took. But finally she made it to the top and stood beside Michael, looking into the distance to see what he saw.

For a long time, as the sun set in an explosion of color, no words were spoken. None were needed.

"You're one of those rare people who knows how to be completely silent and still," said Michael.

"Probably because I spend a lot of time alone."

"By choice?"

"Yes. And you?" she asked.

"I'm a private person. Or used to be. I never expected to be in this position."

"Yusef told me about what happened to your father and brother. I'm so sorry."

Michael nodded. "With their deaths, everything changed. A month ago I was a structural engineer working on a bridge in Egypt. Now I'm ruling a country. Believe me, Jensen, it's not the life I would have chosen for myself."

"What about your brother?"

"He knew from the day he was born that he was to be king. My father made sure that everything in his life, from his education to his fiancée, was geared toward that goal."

"And you?"

"As the younger brother, I was given to my mother to care for, and she chose to raise me in a more American fashion. Over the years, I've spent more time in your country than in my own. Your ways are mine. I even speak better English than Arabic."

"Can't you just walk away?"

"No. Sumaru and its people were my father's responsibility and now they've been passed on to me. I won't dishonor my family by shirking my duties."

Jensen was staring at his profile as he spoke the words. She saw an almost grim determination. And when he turned his head and their eyes met, she saw a great sadness.

Instinctively she reached out to touch his face. He caught her hand in his before it reached his cheek and lowered it to her side. "Lesson number one. Never touch a man when someone might be watching."

"We're in the middle of nowhere."

"There are eyes everywhere," said Michael. "Always assume you're being watched."

"What would be so wrong if someone saw me touch your face?"

"It just isn't done. Besides which, I'm an engaged man. I shouldn't even be talking to you."

"Engaged?" Jensen didn't know why the news hit her so hard, but it did. He was her brother's friend, nothing more. It had nothing to do with her.

"That's right."

"I didn't know."

"But everyone else in my country does." He looked back out at the desert for a moment, then turned to descend the dune. "Ali will have dinner ready."

Jensen tried her best to keep up with him as they made their way down the dune, but she stumbled repeatedly. Michael slowed his pace and took her arm.

Jensen looked at him curiously. "What about that no touching rule of yours?"

"Some chivalry is allowed. Walking in sand takes some getting used to. It's not easy to balance, even for people who have been doing it for years."

Jensen looked around as they walked. "I miss grass," she said. "Trees. And water. Especially water. And I've only been out here for two days."

"You get used to it. The desert has its own beauty."

Jensen thought about what had happened to her earlier. If Michael and Ali hadn't come along when they had, her fate could have been a very different one. "A lethal beauty," she said quietly.

Michael looked down at her. "Like some women."

Chapter Five

When they arrived at the campsite, they found a table set for two with bread, rice, a meat of some sort, sugared dates and a bottle of water, all illuminated by a lantern.

Ali was nowhere in sight, but it was his handiwork. No one else could have done it.

"I'm impressed," said Jensen. "Ferocious, saber wielding and he cooks, too. You're a very lucky man."

Michael suddenly unleashed the smile he'd only hinted at earlier. "Don't let him hear you say that."

"Does he speak English?"

"More than he lets on." Michael waved her onto one of the large pillows Ali had placed near the low table while he sat on the other. As Michael passed food to her, Jensen took a little.

"Eat," said Michael. "It won't hurt you. You've got to be hungry."

"I was. But I think when you go without food long enough, you lose your appetite."

"Take more anyway."

She took a larger helping of the rice and broke off a chunk of bread with her hands. "Is that honey?" she asked of a small dish of tempting golden liquid.

"Yes. Help yourself."

There was no spoon. She tried delicately tilting the bowl so that just a little would fall onto her plate.

Michael smiled as he took the bowl from her, put it on the table, dunked his own bread into it and bit off a chunk. Some honey dripped onto his lips.

Jensen gently wiped it away with her fingertip, then seemingly unconscious of the intimacy of the gesture, raised that finger to her own lips and licked it off.

Michael had to force himself to look down at his plate and focus on his food.

Jensen realized instantly she'd made a mistake and tried to cover it up with conversation. "Where's Ali?" she asked.

"Nearby. He prefers to eat alone."

"Of course."

"You should learn to trust him. He'll be helping us with our search for your brother."

"He doesn't seem like the kind of man who would be someone's bodyguard."

"Why not?"

"Besides being the most frightening man I've ever met, he's also the most dignified."

"To Ali, to be trusted with the guarding of the king is a great honor."

Jensen stared at him.

"What?" said Michael.

"I've never had dinner with a king before. Or are you a sheik?"

"In this instance, the terms are interchangeable."

"What should I call you?"

"Michael."

"Even in public?"

"In public, you won't be addressing me at all."

"Ah, the woman thing."

"That's right. And it's not to be taken lightly. Out here in the desert we can be reasonably casual, but when we're in the public eye you must behave with complete decorum."

Jensen was utterly serious. "I understand. I'll do exactly as you tell me at all times."

"Thank you." He inclined his head toward her plate. "Are you finished?"

"Yes."

"Then you can retire to the tent if you'd like. You'll find some fresh water, a bowl and clean cloths so you can wash. We'll get an early start in the morning."

"Where are you sleeping?"

"Outside."

"And Ali?"

"He always sleeps up on the dune where he has a view of the surrounding desert."

Jensen rose from the pillow and walked into the tent. A lit lantern sat on a small table beside a futonlike cushion that was apparently supposed to be her bed. There was also a basin, soap and a gallon container of water, along with the pack containing her things.

Ali again.

Jensen laid out what she needed and started to undress, then realized she'd forgotten to ask Michael something.

Walking back outside, she softly called his name.

There was no answer.

She walked around to the back of the tent where she saw the dimmest of lights and stopped dead in her tracks.

Michael was there, all right, his back to her, stripped down to a bare nothing, sponging down his body. His broad, bronzed shoulders flowed into a beautifully muscled back and a butt that was made for—well, just about anything one could think of.

Wearing jeans came to mind.

Or wearing nothing at all, for that matter.

He was absolutely beautiful. The most beautiful man she'd ever seen—not that she'd seen very many, to be honest. Better to say he was the most beautiful man she'd ever imagined. Now that gave him quite a bit of competition.

And then, to her chagrin, he turned sideways and she got a whole new view.

Oh, oh, oh. Let's just say the side view lived up completely to the rear view. Nothing disappointing there at all. Quite the contrary.

Whatever question Jensen had intended to ask had completely fled her mind. She turned and, as quietly as she could, made her way back to the tent.

She did the best she could to put the picture of Michael as he was outside out of her mind as she piled her hair on top of her head and stepped out of her clothes.

After pouring water into the basin, she soaked a washcloth, rang it out and wiped it over her face. She could feel the abrasion of the sand on her skin as she wiped it away, then rinsed out the cloth, soaped it and washed her face again, moving the cloth over her throat, the back of her neck, over her arms and breasts and down her body.

Michael had finished and now sat shirtless on a blanket on the sand, looking toward the tent.

He wasn't intentionally spying on her, but Jensen's silhouette was visible through the canvas as the lamp behind her flickered.

He sat mesmerized, watching as Jensen tilted back her head, raised her hand and squeezed water out of the cloth so that it ran down her throat and between her breasts.

With a tightening of his jaw, Michael turned away, lay on his back and stared at the night sky.

Jensen finished washing, then put on the midthigh length man's shirt she wore for pajamas.

Michael turned his head to watch her again as she buttoned the shirt and rolled up the long sleeves. His eyes followed her hand as she reached up and released her hair from its holder, letting it fall in a wave down her back.

She brushed it with long, slow strokes, first over one shoulder and then the other. Suddenly, with the brush halfway down her hair, she just stopped dead still.

Michael raised up on an elbow.

Jensen stared in frozen terror as the brown-and-orange-backed snake slithered across the floor of the tent to within a foot of her. She couldn't scream and knew better than to move.

"Michael," she whispered—or squeaked—knowing perfectly well he couldn't hear her.

Suddenly, seemingly out of nowhere, there was a flash of steel and the now dead snake was pinned to the ground with a dagger.

Jensen looked up expecting to see Ali standing there, but it was Michael.

"Did it bite you?" he asked, clearly worried.

She shook her head.

He picked up the dagger with the snake still impaled on it and threw the reptile through the opening of the tent into the desert beyond.

"Was it poisonous?" asked Jensen.

"Very."

"How do we know if it was alone?"

A corner of his mouth lifted despite the situation. "They don't usually travel in packs."

"Don't laugh at me," she said with a lightly trembling voice that sounded near to tears even as she noticed for the first time he wasn't wearing a shirt.

Michael put his arm around her shoulders and gave her a brotherly hug. "I'm sorry. Everything is all right now. I won't let anything hurt you. Go to bed.''

He started to leave the tent.

"How can you keep anything from hurting me if you're out there and I'm in here?" she asked.

"Go to sleep, Jensen."

"Easy for you to say," she muttered under her breath. "You're the one with the dagger." Jensen checked every corner of the tent before sitting on the ground-level bed and nervously braiding her hair, her gaze flitting here and there.

"Turn out the lantern," said Michael from his blanket outside. "You'll never get to sleep with the light on."

Jensen hesitated a full minute before reaching over and snuffing the light. She lay down and pulled the thin, smooth cover over herself, her eyes wide-open.

Half an hour later, her eyes were still open. "Michael?"

He didn't answer.

"Michael?" she called louder.

"What?"

"I can't sleep. May I come outside with you?"

He let out a long breath as he rose from his blanket and came inside the tent. "Move over."

She scooted to the edge of the cushion. Michael lifted the blanket and slid in beside her, his chest toward her back. "Think you can sleep now?" he asked.

"Do you have your dagger with you?"

"Yes."

She suddenly felt completely safe. "Then yes, I think I can sleep now. Thank you."

"Good night again."

"Night."

There was very little room. Their bodies had no choice but to touch. His body cupped hers. She could feel his warmth against her back and it gave her great comfort. There was nothing sexual about it, though a picture of how he looked without his clothes flashed through her mind.

She pushed it away as quickly as it came.

Well, she tried.

She was almost too tired to think about anything. With an exhausted sigh, Jensen was asleep within minutes.

Michael, though, was wide-awake, his eyes on the back of Jensen's head. He felt the warmth of her body just as she had felt his, but his reaction required restraint to keep his body in check. He didn't want her to feel what she did to him.

And so he began working out complicated mathematical problems in his mind.

Good thing he was an engineer.

He was in a position of trust with Jensen, and he didn't want to do anything to make her uneasier than she already was.

And she was his best friend's little sister.

Though not so very little anymore.

And she smelled wonderful.

Her hair; her skin.

It reminded him of sunshine and fresh air with a

hint of lily. It was unlike any scent he'd ever come across before.

Michael was tired, too, but had to force himself to keep his eyes open. He was afraid that in sleep he would give away what he could control when he was awake.

It was going to be a long night.

She moved against him and Michael, more asleep than awake, was instantly and obviously aroused.

He wrapped her more tightly in his arms and sleepily rubbed his beard shadowed cheek against her hair.

Jensen was having a dream so wonderful she fought against waking. She was thinking that she should remember this for one of her books. It was so completely real she could actually feel the strong, protective arms that held her.

Michael's arms.

She moved her hands down his smoothly muscled back and felt his warmly exhaled breath near her ear.

With her eyes still closed, she kissed his shoulder, then raised her lips to his for a slow, sleepy kiss.

Michael awoke fully in midkiss and pulled away, horrified by what had happened. "Jensen," he said. She sighed and nestled against his body again, her forehead against his throat, her hand resting lightly on his thigh, sound asleep.

Michael froze for a moment before taking her hand from his thigh and raising it to his chest. He lay there for a long time, listening to her breathing;

feeling her body against his, their heat combining and making them both damp.

Math couldn't help him now.

He turned his head for just a moment and rested his lips against her hair, then gently disengaged himself and rose from the cushion to walk to the opening of the tent.

Ali sat a few feet away, legs crossed, back erect, staring into the darkness. Michael left the tent and sat on the sand beside him. "Can't sleep?" he asked.

Ali nodded. "The woman must go."

"I know," said Michael. He could always count on Ali to tell him the absolute truth.

Ali looked at this man he revered above all others. "But you don't want her to."

"What I want doesn't matter. She's here to find her brother. Once that's done, she'll leave."

"But will you be able to let her go?"

"Why do you ask that?"

"I've seen the way you look at her."

"I look at a lot of women."

"Not the way you look at her."

Michael nodded. "I know. She's different. I feel differently about her. Ever since I saw her in that hotel room, it's like she's turned my life upside down. Nothing looks the same or even tastes the same. I haven't stopped thinking about her since that night."

"You can't love her."

"I know."

"Even if you do, you can't. You have obligations

that reach far beyond yourself and your own longings.''

Michael tiredly ran his fingers through his hair. ''I've always been a practical man, Ali. You know that. Emotion has played a very small part in my life.''

''Until this woman,'' said Ali.

Silence fell between them.

''Do you believe in love at first sight?'' Michael asked.

''Yes. But I also believe in taking a long second look.''

''You stole that line.''

A smile cracked Ali's stern countenance. ''I confess it, which makes it no less true. Perhaps what you feel for this Jensen O'Hara is mere desire.''

''There's nothing 'mere' about my desire for Jensen. It very nearly overwhelms me every time I look at her.''

''She's very beautiful.''

''It's more than that.''

Ali nodded. ''I know.''

''You like her, don't you?'' said Michael in surprise.

''Contrary to popular belief,'' said Ali, ''I am human. It would be difficult not to like the woman.''

''If only I'd met her sooner. Even just a few months. Things could be so different.''

''But you didn't, and your destiny is already in motion. There's no changing it now. In eight weeks you will be married and your first order of business will be to produce an heir.''

"First order of business," repeated Michael. "What an appropriate way to phrase it. I'm going to have a child with a woman I barely know and certainly don't love."

"It's the way of our world, Your Highness. You may one day change things, but not soon enough to help you."

"I know. And I accept that." Michael rose from the sand. "Good night, Ali."

Ali rose as well and disappeared into the night.

Michael went back into the tent and stood over Jensen, looking down at her as she slept. With a gentle hand, he pushed her hair away from her damp face, then lifted the silky end of her long braid and held it, rubbing his fingers over it as he watched her, then placing it gently over her breast. He had seen the pictures Henry had carried of her as a child, but he had never imagined her like this.

The muscle in his jaw tightened.

Ali was right. His life was mapped out.

There was no room in it for feelings for Jensen O'Hara.

No room at all.

When Jensen awoke, it was just beginning to get light outside. She lay still, aware that Michael was gone without looking.

Last night had been a revelation. Never before had she felt so completely safe as when he lay beside her.

She was in the best of hands, and if anyone could find Henry, it was Michael.

She turned her head and looked at the indentation on the pillow where his head had lain so close to hers.

Moving slightly, she rested her cheek on it and took a long, deep breath.

It smelled like him; clean and manly.

Closing her eyes, she took another deep breath and slowly let it out. Book after book, she'd created the perfect fictional man.

But Michael wasn't fiction. He was very real, very attractive—and very unavailable.

Opening her eyes, Jensen lay still for a moment before rising. Keeping an eye out for snakes, she sponged herself off and dressed for the day, then tossed her things into her pack and walked out of the tent with it slung over her shoulder.

She stopped suddenly at the sight of Michael standing a few feet away, staring out at the desert.

His long, dark hair was still wet from his own sponge bath. He was naked from the waist up, his bronzed skin almost glowing in the early-morning light.

Her gaze moved up his muscled back to his powerful shoulders and arms and rested there.

"You're up," he said without turning around.

Jensen moved to stand beside him. "How did you know I was behind you?"

"I think there are some people in this world that others are simply aware of."

"In general terms?"

"Oh, no," he said quietly. "In very specific terms." He turned his head and looked at her for a long moment. "I just know where you are without having to see you."

Their gazes locked. It was Jensen who looked away, suddenly uncomfortable. "What time is it?"

"Early. I was just coming to wake you."

Again she looked at him. Things had changed between them since their first meeting. In fact, things had changed dramatically since last night. They were both aware of each other in new ways.

Ways they shouldn't be.

Ways they needed to avoid.

But this time when their gazes locked, Jensen didn't look away; didn't want to.

Michael's gaze moved over her face feature by feature. "Ali has the animals ready."

"What about the tent?"

"It stays where it is. It's a tent, but it's a permanent desert lodging nonetheless."

"I didn't know."

"Do you have your things?"

She indicated her backpack. "Everything I need."

Ali arrived at that moment, his long legs astride one horse and leading the other as well as the camel.

Michael took the pack from Jensen and handed it to Ali, then helped her onto his horse. After sliding a white robe on over his head, he climbed up behind her, their bodies touching intimately.

"Did you sleep well?" he asked as his arms went around her and the horse started forward.

Jensen closed her eyes, her body a mass of sensation as her back was pressed against his chest and his strong thighs cupped hers. She could barely form a coherent thought. "I dreamed a lot," she finally managed to say—and then couldn't shut up. "I don't usually. At least, if I do, I don't remember them in the morning."

"What kind of dreams?"

She turned her head to look at him for a moment and he saw the color rise in her cheeks as she remembered what she thought was a dream of touching him; kissing him.

Michael knew her thoughts exactly.

"Nothing that would interest you," she said firmly.

"You'd be surprised," he said softly against her ear.

Her heart hammered against her breast as she tried desperately to focus on something other than the man whose body was pressed against her own.

Chapter Six

The trip wasn't so bad at first. The desert at dawn wasn't exactly cool, but it was manageable.

But by the time the relentless sun had fully risen, Jensen felt as though her flesh was going to melt. The horse beneath her; Michael's chest behind her; pure heat.

She refused to complain, though. Michael was in the same heat she was in and he was handling it, so she could, too.

And she just knew Ali was waiting for her to fold. Never.

Hours passed with frequent rest and water stops for the horses. They passed very few other people, and those were either riding or leading camels.

Finally there appeared in the wavery distance a

long wall. "Is that your home?" asked Jensen hopefully.

"Yes. We'll be there in half an hour."

Okay, Jensen thought. She could make it for half half an hour. She could survive anything for half an hour.

She watched as they closed in on the wall. It was the color of the sand, but she could see that it was made from great blocks of stone. Beyond the wall rose a palace that was built long and low to the ground except for a few sections that towered three stories.

"The wall," said Michael, "is five hundred years old. Parts of the palace are that old as well, but most of it has been renovated in the past several decades."

"Why is it so far away from any city?"

"It was a fortress in the old days that stood up against invading tribes. Today, it's where we go to get away from everyday things. Our main public home is less than two miles from the hotel where you stayed."

"How many homes do you have?"

"A few, but don't get excited. We aren't as rich as the Gulf Arabs. We don't have oil here. We mine some minerals and other things."

"Do you have your own army?"

"Of course. And air force. Both small but effective."

"You were in the army once, weren't you? I seem to remember Henry saying something about that."

"My brother was in the army. I was in the air force."

"Let me guess," said Jensen. "You were a pilot."

"Yes."

She glanced over her shoulder at him and he smiled at her. Jensen felt as though she'd been given a gift because something told her that this was a man who rarely smiled any longer.

They rode through an open gate in the wall and up to two great, arched, ornately carved wooden doors.

Men appeared from seemingly nowhere to take the horses and camel, completely avoiding looking at Jensen by keeping their eyes lowered to the ground.

She waited for Michael to finish speaking with one of the men and then the two of them, with Ali close behind, walked into the palace.

There was a sudden explosion of color everywhere, from the tiles on the floor to the vaulted and arched ceilings that had been painted like the Sistine Chapel.

"This is the great hall," said Michael. "The paintings you're looking at were done about two hundred years ago. If you go left, you enter the men's quarters. Right is the women's." With his hand in the middle of her back, he steered her toward the right, through another elegant hallway.

"Are you allowed in here?" asked Jensen.

"Of course. But you're not allowed to visit the men's side unless you're specifically invited."

Jensen shook her head, but she didn't say anything.

He opened a door into a brightly lit room full of plants with a small fountain in the middle. The floor was marble and beautiful tapestries hung from the walls.

Huge doors opened into a courtyard that had grass and flowers and another, larger fountain. Two women, one in a modern dress and one in head to toe elaborate robes were seated under a tree reading.

"Nira," said Michael.

Both women looked up.

"Come here, please."

The woman in the dress set her book aside and crossed the courtyard to them. As Jensen watched, she saw Michael and the other woman make very brief eye contact before the woman lowered her lids. Michael inclined his head and the woman did likewise.

"Jensen O'Hara, this is my sister, Nira."

Jensen smiled. Nira didn't. "O'Hara?" she said. "Are you related to Henry?"

"I'm his sister."

"Is Henry with you?"

"No," said Jensen. "He's missing. That's why I'm here."

"Missing? What do you mean, missing?"

"He disappeared from Sumaru," Jensen said. "Michael is going to help me find him."

"Don't ask a lot of questions, Nira," Michael said. "We have a lot to do and not much time to do it in. I need you to take Jensen under your wing for a night. Show her how to dress and behave like a proper Sumaruan woman. Tomorrow I'm taking her to Adjani. We think Henry might be there."

Nira looked at her brother in alarm. "Adjani? She has no place there. You have no place there, either. What are you thinking?"

"You forget yourself, Nira," said her brother in a tone that brooked no argument. "You will do as I ask and help Jensen."

Nira was clearly angry, but she stopped arguing and nodded.

Michael turned toward Jensen. "Please listen carefully to whatever Nira tells you. Your life might depend upon it."

"Michael, I've been thinking."

"That usually means trouble."

"You really are a chauvinist, aren't you?"

"That has nothing to do with chauvinism. It has everything to do with what's happened since we met."

"I'll admit that there have been some problems…"

Michael lifted a dark brow.

Jensen gave him a withering look. "Do you want to hear my idea?"

"You're going to tell me whether I want to or not."

The look turned into a smile. "It's as though you've known me all my life."

"Come on. Out with it."

"Taking me to Adjani is full of problems," she said.

"True."

"I won't be able to go anywhere alone, or go into any of the same places as men. That means I'll be completely dependent on you for everything."

"That's right," agreed Michael.

"But that all changes if I go as a man instead of a woman."

He gave her a single Clint Eastwood-like blink. "A man?"

"Exactly. As a woman, I'm powerless. As a man, I'm on an equal footing with you."

Michael reached out and touched her cheek then let his hand fall away. "By what magic am I to transform these delicate features into those of a man?" His gaze moved down her body, but not in an offensive way. "Not to mention the rest of you."

"I won't wear any makeup."

"You aren't wearing any now and, believe me, you don't look anything like a man."

Nira looked from Michael to Jensen and back to her brother. What was going on here?

"It's not a bad idea, though," Michael said. "You'd be less conspicuous as a man. And you'd probably be safer. What do you think, Nira? Can you make her look like a man?"

She walked around Jensen, giving her the once-over and stopping in front of her, arms crossed. "As far as her figure, we can bind her so that she isn't as curved. The robes will cover the rest. And we can artificially darken her skin. If she wears the cloth of the headdress forward, it will cover her profile. And her hair, of course, will be hidden."

Michael shook his head. "I don't know."

"Well, I do," said Nira. "Let the women handle this." She gave Michael a little shove. "Leave us now. We have a lot of work to do and only one night to do it in."

He turned back to Jensen. "We leave early, by car."

"I'll be ready."

He leaned over and kissed the top of his sister's head. "Thank you, Nira." Then he looked at the woman across the way and inclined his head again before leaving.

"Who is she?" asked Jensen, assuming the woman was another sister.

"Ayalah, Michael's fiancée."

Jensen looked at Nira in surprise. "His fiancée? Then why did they greet each other so coolly?"

"Come," said Nira as she stook Jensen's arm and led her into the palace. "It's a long and unhappy story. I'll tell you when you've finished bathing."

She signaled some women who were standing nearby and spoke to them in Arabic. They instantly went in separate directions while Nira took Jensen to a large tiled room with a sunken mosaic bath large enough to hold four people.

One of the women, who had followed them, turned on a faucet and water began spilling into the tub. Another woman came in and added a jasmine fragrance from a glass pitcher.

"I'll see you shortly," said Nira. "Enjoy your bath. It's the last one you'll be having until you return."

When Nira had gone, one of the women held up a bright red cloth while the other helped Jensen out of her clothes. Jensen tried to send them away, but she spoke no Arabic and they spoke no English.

Jensen had no choice but to set aside her natural modesty. Taking the two steps down into the bath, she sank into the warm, fragrant water with a sigh of pleasure that spread through her entire body. She ducked her head in the water, wetting her face and hair.

A woman knelt behind Jensen above the bath and soaped her hair, then poured pitcher after pitcher of water over it until all of the soap was gone.

Once she was out of the bath, she was wrapped in yards of cloth and placed on a cushion while her hair was brushed out. The cloth was then taken away and replaced by a robe.

Nira walked in just as Jensen finished. "All clean," she said with satisfaction. "Are you hungry?" she asked.

"Starving!"

Nira took Jensen's hand and led her to a small room with a low table set with at least a dozen small bowls, each holding some delicacy. They sat on cushions across from each other. "Please," said Nira, "enjoy. If you want anything else, you have but to ask."

"What about Ayalah?"

"She's not permitted to socialize at the moment."

"Oh. I thought perhaps she was with Michael."

"Heavens no."

"Why do you say it like that? If they're engaged, it would be only natural."

"They've never spoken."

"I don't understand."

"She was originally engaged to our older brother. It was not a love match, but a matter of politics." Nira's eyes filled with a sudden sorrow. "As you may know, he was killed recently and now it falls upon Michael to marry her."

Jensen couldn't believe what she was hearing. "You can't mean it. That's barbaric."

Nira shrugged. "Perhaps, but that's the way it is. Michael understands his duty and he is the kind of man who will always do the honorable thing." She looked at Jensen for a long moment. "Regardless of what his own desires might be."

"How will he ever find happiness?"

"There are options for men in Michael's position. If he finds himself in love with a woman, he can take her for his mistress and have children with her. They won't be in the line of succession, but they would certainly be well cared for."

"What kind of woman would be willing to do that? If one loves a man, she loves him completely. Sharing him with another woman would be absolutely unthinkable."

"What if there were no other way to be with him?"

"But there would have to be."

Nira shook her head. "Whoever falls in love with Michael must be willing to accept what he is able to offer or will have to stay out of his life altogether.''

"What about his fiancée? Doesn't she have any say in her own future?''

"None at all.''

"I don't understand this.''

"You used to have arranged marriages in America. In some cases, you still do. This is no different.''

"Times have changed.''

"Not here. Not for us.''

"But your mother was American. She couldn't have approved of marrying her sons to women they don't love.''

"She didn't. But she didn't live long enough to bring about any real change. And my father didn't have the strength to do it without her by his side.''

"And you, Nira? Will the same thing happen to you? Will you be married off to some man you don't love?''

"Anything is possible, but I don't think so. It falls upon Michael to make those decisions for his family now, and he would never ask me to marry where there was no love. Unfortunately, there's nothing he can do to save himself. Or his fiancée for that matter.''

Jensen's appetite had deserted her completely. "Perhaps they'll fall in love after their marriage.''

"That sometimes happens,'' said Nira. "She's certainly a nice enough sort of woman. And who wouldn't fall in love with Michael? He's the best of men.''

"Yes," she agreed. "He seems to be. How did your father manage to break ranks and marry an American?"

"Like Michael, he was the younger son. He married our mother before becoming king."

"I see."

"Had he been the older son, or become king before marriage to our mother, he would have been obliged to choose someone very different for his wife."

"And would he have?"

"He would have done his duty." Nira reached out and touched Jensen's hand. "Don't fall in love with Michael. I can tell you now that whatever his heart urges him to do, his duty will win in the end. He will always do what's required of him, what's best for the country. That's just the way he is."

"What makes you think I'm in danger of falling in love with your brother?" asked Jensen uneasily.

"All one has to do is watch the way you look at him."

"He's a handsome man. Any woman would enjoy looking at him."

"But there's more in your eyes than simple enjoyment of an object of beauty. And there's more in his eyes when he looks at you. I fear for both of you if you don't stay in control of your emotions."

"I can't imagine Michael out of control," Jensen said.

"I couldn't, either, until a couple of hours ago." She sighed. "But enough of that. I've sent someone to bring you some men's robes. We'll get you fitted this evening so you'll be ready to go first thing in the morning.''

"Fitted?''

"In length. The headdress, of course, won't be a problem. And I have some stain that we'll use on your skin to darken it.''

"Why stain?''

"Makeup will never do. It rubs off, particularly in this heat. A stain is much better.''

"But will it come off?''

"In time. But it will require some serious scrubbing.'' She pointed at Jensen's plate. "You aren't eating.''

Jensen took a halfhearted bite.

"What's the matter?''

"I'm worried about my brother. I don't know what I'll do if anything has happened to Henry. I love him. He's the only family I have.''

Nira nodded. "I like your brother very much. He's a good man. My oldest brother was a good man, too.''

"Oh,'' said Jensen as she touched Nira's hand. "I'm sorry. You've been so kind I forgot what you've been through.''

Nira's eyes filled with tears, but she quickly wiped them away. "I've cried a river, but then I remind myself that it could have been worse. Michael was supposed to be on the plane that crashed as well as my father and other brother.''

Jensen's heart caught in a way that was completely unexpected. "Michael?''

"He was late getting to the airport. My father, an

impatient man at the best of times, decided not to wait and told the pilot to take off without him. Imagine what would have happened if he hadn't?''

Jensen didn't want to imagine. It was too horrible a thought to contemplate.

A woman walked in, her arms loaded with clothing. Nira smiled. ''Ah, it's time to experiment.''

Nira took the lead as she and the other woman led Jensen to a room. ''This will be your quarters for the evening.''

She signaled to the other woman and spoke to her in Arabic. The woman began carefully spreading the clothing out on the bed.

''Here we go,'' said Nira, as she picked up what looked like a back brace that fastened in the front with Velcro. ''Wrap this around your breasts.''

Jensen, quickly losing her modesty in this world of women, let the silken robe she was wearing slide to the floor and bound herself with the brace as tightly as she could.

Nira looked at her and nodded. ''Now, let's try the robe.'' Both women slipped the soft white cotton over Jensen's head and buttoned it up the front. Yards of material billowed around her and touched the floor. The other woman knelt on the floor and began pinning up the material. ''We won't take it up too much,'' said Nira. ''We don't want your ankles to show.''

Nira walked around her. ''Now for your hair.'' She took a brush from a nearby table and ran it through Jensen's hair, then expertly braided it and twisted it around Jensen's head, holding the whole thing in place with a single pin.

"This is the bottom piece of the headdress," she said as she placed a white circlet on Jensen's head. "Then we place the scarf on top of that," she explained as she did it, arranging it artfully around Jensen's face, "and then, to hold everything in place is the ogal." She took a thick black cloth band from the bed and put it on top of Jensen's head, then stepped back to look at her handiwork. "Not bad, if I do say so myself. Just make sure you keep the scarf around your face as much as possible."

"I will."

"All that's left is to stain your skin."

The woman on the floor rose and lifted the robe over Jensen's head, then removed the headgear and placed it on the bed. There was a ripping sound as Jensen undid the Velcro fastener on the brace.

Nira handed the other woman a bottle and cloth that had been on a table in the corner. "This won't harm your skin," she assured her as the other woman began applying the stain in long, smooth strokes to Jensen's legs and arms. "Some women here use it to enhance their own natural color."

"Do I need it all over?"

"I think you should."

And so Jensen stood still as she was stained all over with the beautiful walnut-colored liquid.

When it was over, she turned to look in the mirror and could hardly believe what she saw. If she hadn't known better, she would have thought this lovely color was natural.

Nira smiled at her. "It looks wonderful with your hair."

"Thank you. I like it," said Jensen as she picked up the silken robe she'd had on earlier and put it on.

Nira spoke in Arabic to the other woman, who collected the men's garments and left. "They'll be ready for you in the morning," she told Jensen. "And now, I'll leave you to get sleep. You have a difficult journey ahead of you."

Jensen turned to Nira and smiled. "Thank you for everything."

On an impulse, Nira hugged her. "Good luck with your search. I'll be waiting anxiously for word of Henry."

"Oh, Henry," Jensen whispered when Nira had gone. "You have to be all right. What will I do if you're not?"

Chapter Seven

Jensen turned out the lights almost as soon as Nira was gone, but she didn't go to bed. Instead, she stood in the doorway of the room and looked out at the courtyard.

Did all of the main rooms of the palace look out on courtyards? she wondered.

The night air was cool; inviting.

Jensen's nerves wouldn't let her sleep.

Barefoot, she entered the courtyard and walked round the garden, smelling the roses and jasmine.

Michael stood in a darkened room at the far end that had served as his father's study. It was the only courtyard in the palace that accommodated both a room from the men's section and the women's section. His mother had designed it.

He watched as Jensen moved among the flowers, bending occasionally to inhale their fragrance.

Sitting on a bench, she pulled the pin out and let the long braid fall. With her fingers, she brushed through her hair until it fell softly around her, then sat still, deep in thought.

Michael couldn't take his eyes from her.

Didn't want to.

And so he stayed where he was, watching this woman who had so unexpectedly come into his life.

This woman he shouldn't want.

This woman he could never have.

He turned away and walked back into the room.

Jensen lay on the bench and stared at the sky. All kinds of thoughts were running through her mind. Thoughts she didn't want to have; thoughts she didn't want to deal with.

She fell asleep where she lay.

And she dreamed.

Jensen was running through narrow streets as fast as she could, trying to get away. She kept looking over her shoulder to see if it was gaining on her. She couldn't see anything, but knew it was there—a presence...an evil presence. And even as she ran, faster and faster, in her heart she knew there was no escape.

The wall came from nowhere. It just suddenly appeared in front of her. She searched frantically for a way through it or around it, her hands clawing at the bricks until they were broken and bloody, but there was none. She was cornered.

With her back pressed flat against it, she waited

for the end. She could feel it coming closer and closer...

Jensen sat straight up, her heart pounding, her breath coming in painful gasps. A film of perspiration covered her from head to toe.

She sat where she was, leaning her head against the back of the bench, gulping deep breaths of the night air. She gradually calmed down, but something of the fear stayed with her, even though she knew it was only a dream.

She couldn't shake it.

Raising her head, she began looking around and saw a lighted room across the courtyard.

Someone else was awake. Nira, perhaps. Wrapping herself in her robe, she walked barefoot across the courtyard to the open doors. It wasn't a bedroom, as she'd thought, but a library.

And Michael was there, not Nira.

He was dressed in jeans and a striped shirt, sitting behind a desk, his elbows on the top, his head in his hands.

She might have turned and walked away except for that.

Jensen's heart caught at the sight. "Michael," she said softly.

He turned away from her. "Go back to bed, Jensen."

She came closer and he put his hand up as if to ward her away. "Please, go."

Jensen knelt by his chair and took his face in her soft, cool hands. "Talk to me."

"Talking isn't going to help."

She kissed his cheek.

"Jensen..."

She kissed his other cheek. All she wanted to do was erase that look of pain from his face.

With a groan, he grasped the back of her head and crushed her lips to his.

After her initial surprise, Jensen opened herself to him. She couldn't help it.

The urgent passion of the kiss turned to a gentle exploration that ached with longing.

Michael was the one who stopped. He tangled his fingers in her hair and leaned his forehead against hers. "You caught me at a weak moment. I'm sorry."

"It's all right. I understand."

He kissed her forehead, then rose and walked away from her.

Jensen stayed where she was. "What were you thinking about when I came in?"

Michael didn't answer for a long time. "My brother was only two years older than I am. And my father was still a young man with great ideas about how the country should be run. They both needed more time to bring our people into the twentieth century. It isn't right that they're gone."

Jensen rose from the floor and stood behind Michael, her hands on his shoulders. "You can do for your people what your father and brother would have done."

"My father was the one with the vision. My brother was raised to be a king. I'm an engineer.

That's all I ever wanted to be. It's what I'm trained for.''

"Then be an engineer. You don't have to be king, do you?''

"You're right. I could walk away.''

"But you won't,'' she guessed.

"My father might not have trained me to be a king, but he and my mother did train me to take responsibility. This country is my responsibility. The people are depending on me to guide them and to provide a strong enough leadership to keep them from being swallowed up by neighboring countries. I'll do what I have to.''

"Including marrying a woman you don't love?''

He turned to look at Jensen. "Yes.''

"Why?''

"Because that's the way things have to be.''

Their gazes locked.

Jensen blinked first. "I'm sorry. I'm intruding into areas where I clearly have no business. I should never have barged in here.'' She started to walk past him and out the door.

"Don't go,'' he said softly. "Stay with me.''

Jensen stopped.

"Just for a little while.''

She let out a long breath.

"What's wrong?''

"I had no business coming to you for help about Henry. You have enough on your mind without my adding to it. I didn't know all that had happened to you.''

"It doesn't matter. Henry is my friend. Of course I want to help find him."

"What you want to do and what you ought to be doing are two different things. This is no time for your attention to be split. I can figure out something. Get someone…"

"Like the guide you thought was sent by the embassy?"

"That was a mistake."

"A mistake that nearly cost you your life. That's not a risk I'm willing to take any longer."

"This is my life we're talking about. My risk."

He looked at her for a long moment. "I'm not backing away from this, Jensen. We're going to find Henry together."

"Whatever the cost?"

"Yes." His voice was almost a whisper.

"I think I could fall in love with you." Jensen hadn't meant to say it, but there it was. The words were between them.

"And I've been in love with you from the moment I saw you in the hotel."

Their eyes met and held.

"So what do we do?" asked Jensen. "Where do we go from here?"

"We find Henry. Then you go back to Wisconsin and I come back here."

"What if I can't let you go?"

"You'll have to. We'll have to. But Henry comes before anything else. I can help you find him. I have better resources than any guide you'll be able to hire. And I can keep you safe."

"You're right," she agreed reluctantly. "We'll do it your way."

"And tomorrow we'll blame this conversation on the lateness of the hour and the exhaustion of the participants."

Jensen attempted a smile.

Michael was determined to change the subject. He inclined his head toward her. "I admit it's a nice tan, but you still don't look anything like a man."

"Ah, you haven't seen me in my new clothes. Rarely has the world seen so much manliness in one package. Even Ali will be impressed." She walked around the study. It was all arches, bookcases, leather and tapestries. "This is a wonderful room."

"It was one of my father's favorites. Mine, too."

"I'm surprised to find it just across the courtyard from the women's quarters."

"My mother designed it that way. There were certain customs she refused to follow. One of them was being separated from my father. This area was a place where they could be together in complete privacy. Only their bedrooms and this study face the courtyard."

"I wouldn't agree to be separated from my husband, either, regardless of what the custom was."

"And I can't imagine your husband agreeing to be separated from you."

Jensen smiled at him. She couldn't help it. "We're in for a tough time of it."

"I know. You'd better go to bed, Jensen. We'll be leaving in a few hours."

She headed toward the door. "Michael?" she said without turning.

"Yes?"

"Thank you for everything you're doing. I might not always act like it, but I'm grateful to you. Good night."

Michael watched her walk away and continued to watch her until she was safely in her room.

Jensen, both physically and emotionally exhausted, fell asleep as soon as her head hit the pillow.

The next time she opened her eyes, Michael was there.

"It's dawn," he said softly. "Get dressed. I'll meet you in the courtyard."

Jensen was instantly alert. "I'll just be a few minutes."

As quickly as she could, she found her way to the bath, brushed her teeth and rinsed her face.

The stain held, she noted with satisfaction.

Then she dressed in her new clothes the servant had returned during the night, and looked at herself in a long mirror.

The clothes worked, but she was still very feminine looking. Perhaps it was the way she carried herself; the way she moved.

She was just going to have to be more guylike.

Adding what she thought was a strut to her walk, she went back to her room for her backpack and met Michael in the courtyard.

As soon as he saw her, he had to smile.

"What?" she asked. "I think I look pretty good. And I'll have the walk down before we get there."

"You don't have a masculine bone in your body."

"You wouldn't say that if you could see me play touch football with Henry and his friends."

"Yes, I would, but be that as it may, let's go."

"You're not ready," she said, inclining her head toward his cotton khaki trousers and white T-shirt.

"I'm more comfortable in these. I'll put my other clothes on when we get closer to Adjani."

With his hand in the middle of her back, Michael guided her through the palace to the two cars that awaited them in the driveway. Jensen stopped and stared at the rattletraps that were old Hummers with paint pitted from years in the desert.

"You can't be serious," she said. "These won't get us ten miles much less all the way to Adjani."

"They'll get us to Adjani and back."

"Why two?"

"To carry extra water and fuel—and to be on the safe side in case one breaks down."

Ali appeared suddenly and silently beside them.

Jensen gasped and put her hand over her heart. "I wish you'd make at least the occasional noise," she told him.

Ali just looked at her.

But Jensen was unfazed by his silence. She stepped back and did a turn. "What do you think, Ali? Will I pass for a man? Michael doesn't seem to think so."

There was no change of expression.

Jensen sighed. "Which—car—do you want me in?"

Michael had intended putting her in with Ali, but relented. "Come with me."

Moments later, they were on their way. For the first hour or so there was something resembling a road, but that soon turned into a track that had holes and rocks. They couldn't have been traveling more than twenty miles an hour, if that, and were churning up sand all the way.

An added bonus was the constant heat.

Jensen took off her headdress and tossed it into the back. "How can you stand to wear these things?"

"They protect us from the sun. And you from prying eyes."

"Let me know a bit before we reach Adjani. I'll put it back on."

Michael looked at her profile. "Talk to me about yourself?"

"What?" she asked in surprise.

"I know very little about you except what Henry's told me over the years."

"There's not much to tell. I'm a writer. I spend my days at a computer in an office in my home."

"Do you live alone?"

"No."

"So you live with someone?"

Jensen smiled. "My home is an old farmhouse that I share with a very large dog."

"There's no man in your life?"

"That's right."

"Then where do you get your ideas of love, adventure and romance for your books?"

"Let's just say that I live a very rich fictional life."

"What about your real life?"

Jensen thought for a moment before answering. "I like it. It's comfortable and safe—and green!" she joked.

"And do you like being alone?"

"Actually, yes."

"You surprise me."

"Why?"

"You're a beautiful woman. I would have thought there would be many men knocking on your door."

"As I said, I live in a farmhouse in Wisconsin. My town has all of fifteen hundred people in it. The only men who come knocking on my door are the ones who fix plumbing."

Michael laughed out loud.

"That's nice," said Jensen.

"What is?"

"Your laugh. That's the first time I've heard it since we met. You should do it more often."

"Henry and I used to laugh all of the time."

"Everyone laughs when they're with Henry."

"That's one of the things I liked best about him when we were in college. That and the fact that he was never intimidated by who my father was."

"He's always been like that. I think that's why he's such a good journalist. No one particularly impresses him above anyone else. He treats everyone the same way."

"Are you intimidated?" asked Michael.

"By you?"

"Not by me as a man, but by my position."

"How honest should I be?"

"As honest as you can."

"Then I'd have to say that I'm a bit like Henry in that I'm not intimidated by your position. And I'm not usually intimidated by people, but I am a little by you."

"Why?"

Jensen couldn't help smiling. "How far do you want me to go with this? Keep in mind that I analyze relationships for a living and can go on and on."

"We have hours of driving ahead of us."

"You asked for it. I've always been predisposed to like you because of Henry. But when he disappeared and I thought you weren't going to help me find him, I didn't like you. Then I met you and I decided I *really* didn't like you at all."

"Ouch."

"Well, you attacked me!"

He held up his hand where her teeth marks were still clearly visible. "For your viewing pleasure," he said.

"Self-defense." She took his hand in hers and examined it more closely. "I'm really sorry, Michael. I panic when anything gets put over my face and I was told in a self-defense course that I took that biting was perfectly permissible if we were attacked."

"That's all right. It's nice to know you can take care of yourself. Besides, it'll give me something to remember you by years from now when I look at the scar.''

She put his hand back on the gearshift between them.

"Go on," he said.

Jensen thought about her next words, but decided to say them anyway. "I feel as though I've gotten to know you better over the past few days. I've had some glimpses, I think, into your soul. You're a man capable of great love for family and loyalty toward friends. You're a man of duty and honor, all qualities I admire and find in others, male and female, all too infrequently." She turned her head to look at him. "Everything about you attracts me, from your character to your blue eyes. If circumstances were different..." She shrugged. "But they aren't."

Michael's hand tightened on the gearshift.

"How's that for analytical honesty?" she asked.

"Last night when we were talking, you said you could have loved me. Could have. How do you keep feelings for someone in the 'could have' range?"

"Interesting question," said Jensen. She was trying very hard to keep the emotion out of the conversation. "I don't know. I've never had to deal with that before."

"You've never been in love?"

"I don't think so. Not real love. Have you?"

"No."

"You say that with great certainty."

"I've been attracted to, fond of, in like of and in lust with women. Not in love."

She was thinking about the woman at the palace.

"Was your brother in love with the woman he was going to marry?"

"No," said Michael softly, "he wasn't."

"How do you feel about her?"

"I see you've been talking to my sister."

"You handed me over to her. It was kind of hard not to."

He nodded. "Well, I feel sad for her. And I feel sad for me. But neither of us really has a choice in the matter."

"What would happen if one of you simply refused to marry the other one?"

"That would never happen."

"Why?"

"If I refused to marry her, it would dishonor both my father and brother. If she were to refuse to marry me, she would be dishonoring her family and would probably be cast out from them."

"Can either of you ever be happy?"

"Not happy. But perhaps we'll find some measure of contentment as the years pass."

"Will that be enough?"

Michael turned his head and looked at Jensen for a long moment. "It will have to be, won't it?"

"Will you have mistresses?"

Michael chuckled, a delicious sound from deep within. "You ask the most amazing questions. I can't believe I'm even having this conversation with you."

"Do you mind?"

"Oddly enough, I don't. I'm usually an extremely

private person about my thoughts and feelings, but talking to you about them seems quite natural.''

Jensen smiled at him. ''Then I'll repeat my impertinent question. Will you have mistresses?''

''I don't know. I never would have thought so, but that was when I expected to marry a woman I loved. I don't know how I'll feel in the years to come, or who I'll meet.''

''Did your father have mistresses?''

''No. Never. Not even after my mother died. He loved her completely. What about you? Will you take lovers?''

''Not if I'm married. I can't imagine wanting to if I was truly in love, and I would never marry anyone I didn't love.''

''All marriages have rough patches.''

''I know. But if the basic foundation of the marriage isn't trust, rough patch or not, then there's nothing there to begin with.''

Michael had turned off what little road there had been a long time before. They were truly driving in the desert.

''How do you know where you're going?'' asked Jensen. ''There are no signs, no stores, no landmarks.''

''There are landmarks. You just don't see them because they aren't familiar to you.''

''For example?''

''The dune you see about fifteen miles to our left.''

''A dune is a dune.''

''That's not true, Jensen. Some remain essentially

unchanged for centuries. Like that one. And there are tracks under the coating of sand we're riding on.''

"How can you see them?"

"They're faint but they're there. We're not the only ones who go to Adjani.''

"Are you thirsty?" she asked.

"Yes."

She unbuckled her seat belt and stretched between their seats to pick up a liter bottle of water from the rear. She saw Ali close on their bumper and waved at him.

No response.

Back in her seat, she opened the bottle and handed it to Michael. He took a long drink and gave it back to her. She drank some, too, then poured a little into her hand and dabbed it on her face and throat.

Without his asking, Jensen poured some more onto her fingers and reached over to dab some on Michael's throat.

As soon as she touched him, his hand shot up and caught her wrist to pull it away.

"I'm sorry," she said in surprise. "I thought you must be hot, too. I was just trying to cool you off a little."

He put her hand in her lap. "I am."

"What did I do wrong?"

"Nothing, Jensen. It's me. Just don't touch me."

"I wasn't thinking."

Michael squeezed her hand before freeing it. "It's

all right. We just need to be careful and think before we act.''

''I will.''

He glanced at her. ''We'll get through this, you know.''

Jensen nodded. ''I know.''

Chapter Eight

Jensen's head turned as they passed a deserted car
on the side of their track road.

"That's why we brought two cars," Michael said.

"What happened to the people who were in it?"

"Either someone came along to help them, or
they died in the desert from exposure."

"Maybe they had enough water to make it to the
next town," said Jensen hopefully.

"This road leads only to Adjani."

The farther they went, the more deserted cars they
saw, peopling the desert like mechanical ghosts.

"How does a place like Adjani come into being?"

"It's existed for more than a thousand years. It's
a place for outlaws, like some towns in your West
were a hundred years ago."

"Can't it be cleaned up?"

"It's been tried."

"Can't you occupy it with troops?"

"Adjani isn't part of my country or I'm sure my father would have taken care of it a long time ago."

"I'm embarrassed. I should have looked at a map before venturing out here."

"Understand, Jensen, that I have to be circumspect in looking for Henry in Adjani. I sent a few men there unofficially. I've made no official inquiry because I don't trust the government there to tell me the truth, and I don't want to alert them to Henry's presence in any way if he's there and in disguise or hiding. They don't like journalists. It's to their benefit to keep the things that happen in Adjani as quiet as possible."

She nodded. "I hope he's there. I don't know where I'll look next if he's not."

"You'll go back to America and let me look."

"I don't go home unless Henry goes with me."

Michael smiled.

"What?"

"He said you were always trying to mother him, even though he was six years older than you."

"Henry needed mothering and still does." Her eyes moved over his profile. "You don't though. In fact, I bet you took care of Henry when you were in school, getting him out of scrapes, making sure he got his work done."

"Henry was a hell-raiser back then. He still is."

"And you weren't." It wasn't a question.

"I tended to be more of a nonjudgmental watcher

than a participant. That's why we got along so well."

"I wish I'd known you. Why didn't you ever come home with Henry for vacations?"

"I had other obligations. My time wasn't my own during holidays."

"Of course."

He suddenly downshifted and stopped the car. "Time to gas up," he said. "You have a few minutes to stretch your legs."

While she walked around, Michael unloaded some five-gallon containers of diesel fuel and poured them into the tank. Ali did the same thing.

Jensen lifted her robe a little and swirled it around to create some air movement. "How long before we arrive in Adjani?"

"Two hours," said Michael. "Perhaps a little less."

He finished pouring the fuel and loaded the containers back into the car.

Jensen started practicing her walk again.

Michael watched with a slight smile curving his lips. "Hit the ground harder with your feet. You're moving too delicately."

She walked back and forth.

"Longer strides," he told her.

"Oh, yeah," she said, "I'm definitely feeling more guylike."

Ali watched her for a moment, then looked at Michael with an expression that would have included rolling eyes, if Ali were the kind of man to do something like that. It was the first really human emotion Jensen had seen cross his face.

She strolled over to them. "Making fun of me isn't going to help."

"We're not making fun," said Michael, trying desperately not to smile. "Your walk is better than it was. But this face," he said, reaching out and touching her smooth cheek, "isn't going to fool anyone, even with darkened skin."

"Perhaps a false beard?" she suggested.

"I just happen to have one in the glove compartment," said Michael dryly.

Ali said something in Arabic.

Michael nodded his head and leaned into his car in search of something. He came back out, triumphant, a pair of men's sunglasses in his hand. "These were my brother's," he said as he slipped them on her nose. "Now put on your headdress."

She reached in and took it from the back seat, but had some trouble getting it on correctly.

Ali came up behind her and put everything in place—very firmly in place—then the two men stood back, arms crossed, and gave her the once-over.

Ali gave her a long look then again spoke to Michael in Arabic before striding back to his car.

"What did he say?" asked Jensen.

"That he thinks you're crazy to do this and I'm crazy for letting you. You're still too pretty for a man."

Jensen looked at him skeptically. "Ali told you, his king, that he thinks you're crazy?"

"Ali doesn't speak often, but when he does, it's always the absolute truth. Even to me."

"I respect that," said Jensen. She walked over to Ali's car and leaned her arms on the open window.

Ali, behind the steering wheel, looked straight ahead as though she wasn't there.

"You know," she said, "before this is over, you're going to like me. I've made up my mind to it, and whenever I do that, things become inevitable. Brace yourself, big fella."

As she walked away, Ali's eyes followed her. He didn't actually smile, but his mouth twitched.

This time, Jensen left the headdress and the sunglasses on as they drove, and she stopped asking Michael questions. It was time to be quiet and think about what lay ahead.

Then the walls of the city came into view and Jensen felt her stomach knot.

This wasn't a game.

This was life and death.

As they approached the walled city, Jensen was struck by how well it blended in with its surroundings. So much so that it looked like it was part of the desert.

But then everything was beginning to look that way to her. There was a sameness about everything.

They had seen only the occasional car, even as they neared the city, but as they took the road into the city, traffic picked up considerably. All kinds of traffic. Camels, horses, cars, people on foot. The streets were packed.

And the smell. It was distinctive and invasive. A

combination of spicy food, body sweat, fragrance to mask the body odor and animals.

The sidewalks were thick with people. Cars barely fit on the narrow, winding, dirt streets. Dust hung suspended in the air, visible in the bright sunlight.

It was burningly hot and still Jensen shivered. There was something sinister about the place.

And she was certain she would have felt that way even if no one had told her a thing about it.

No one looked at them as they drove past. It was as though everyone was determined to mind his own business.

Michael stopped in front of a building without any signage—a run-down vision of cracked stone and peeling paint—and parked in front of it.

"Wait here," he said. "I'll be right back."

Ali parked immediately behind them and took up a stance near the doorway just a few feet from Jensen so he could apparently see both Michael and her.

Jensen watched the street in surprise. "Where do all of these nice cars come from? This looks like such a dirt-poor town." She didn't expect Ali to either understand what she was saying or respond.

"They're trucked or flown in."

She looked at him in surprise but didn't remark. The man's English was flawless. "Flown?"

"There's a small airstrip nearby that belongs to the sheik of Adjani. He allows it to be used occasionally, for a hefty fee, of course."

"Who owns all these cars?"

"Criminals. And, of course, buyers who have come for the white slave auction."

Just the thought of something like that made her stomach knot. "How often do they have these auctions?"

"Twice a year. It's always a big event. People come from around the world."

Michael walked out the door and climbed into the car.

"Where are we going?" asked Jensen.

"I've arranged for us to rent a place on the edge of town."

"Why can't we just stay at a hotel?"

"There's only one, and it's no place for a lady."

"I don't care about that."

"Do you like bugs?"

"No."

"And I think we already know how you feel about snakes."

"I'd say you'd had an indication, yes."

"And thieves in the night?"

"Oh, well, thieves," she said dryly. "They're better than snakes."

Michael tossed her a look. "Trust my judgment on this. We won't be in the lap of luxury, but I've rented a decent place where you'll be safe from harm."

"How is that going to help us find my brother?"

"It neither helps nor hinders us, Jensen." Michael suddenly reached over and squeezed her hand. "If Henry is here, we'll find him. I promise you this."

Jensen nodded. She believed him completely. Michael would never promise anything he couldn't back up.

They traveled less than a mile to a small beige house set on a small beige hill.

Michael parked in front with Ali right behind him. While Michael unloaded some things from the car, Ali went inside and looked around, came back out and nodded his head, giving them, apparently, the all clear.

Michael carried some things inside and Jensen grabbed her backpack and followed him.

It was actually kind of pretty, with bright tiles on the floors and, in some cases, on the walls. After the nearly empty foyer, there was a living room with low couches loaded with colorful pillows set in a circular pattern. There were three separate bedrooms, and Michael looked at all three before walking into one and signaling her to follow.

"This one is yours. The bed linens are fresh. Our rooms share a bathroom. There's running water, but limited use. And, whatever you do, don't drink it. If you get thirsty, there's plenty of bottled water in the kitchen or the cars. And that includes brushing your teeth or eating anything washed in the water."

"All right."

"Ali is going to bring us some food. Any requests?"

Jensen smiled beatifically. "Oh, yes. I'd just like a sandwich. A nice, plain turkey sandwich on nice plain bread. White bread. And a soda." She thought for a moment. "And potato chips."

"Healthy little devil, aren't you?"

"And apple pie for dessert," she added for good measure.

"Right. I'll tell him."

A corner of her mouth lifted. "There's no way I'm going to get turkey, is there?"

"No way."

She sighed.

"Maybe chicken."

"And apple pie?"

He shook his head. "Sorry."

"Potato chips?"

"Those we have."

"Just tell him I'll take whatever he can find. And while Ali is looking for food, what do we do? Go looking for Henry?"

"No. You're going to wait here."

"What about you?"

"I have other things to do."

"Michael...."

"I'm going to meet with the two men I sent here a couple of days ago later tonight. You stay here. I'll let you know what they say."

"I wish you'd stop trying to protect me."

"Henry would never forgive me if I let anything happen to his little sister."

"And I really, really wish you'd stop thinking of me as Henry's little sister."

His eyes met and held hers. "How would you like me to think of you, Jensen?"

Her heart began hammering a rapid beat. "I could be wrong. Perhaps Henry's little sister is the safest."

Michael's gaze moved from her eyes to her mouth. "Clean up and I'll meet you in the living room."

PLAY "LUCKY 7" AND GET
THREE FREE GIFTS!

HOW TO PLAY:

1. With a coin, carefully scratch off the silver box at the right. Then check the claim chart to see what we have for you — **FREE BOOKS** and a gift — **ALL YOURS! ALL FREE!**

2. Send back this card and you'll receive brand-new Silhouette Special Edition® novels. These books have a cover price of $4.25 each, but they are yours to keep absolutely free

3. There's no catch. You're under no obligation to buy anything. We charge nothing — ZERO — for your first shipmen And you don't have to make any minimum number of purchases — not even one!

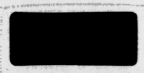

4. The fact is thousands of readers enjoy receiving books by mail from the Silhouette Reader Service™ months before they're available in stores. They like the convenience of home delivery and they love our discount prices!

5. We hope that after receiving your free books you'll want to remain a subscriber. But the choice is yours — to continue or cancel, any time at all! So why not take us up on o invitation, with no risk of any kind. You'll be glad you did!

YOURS FREE!

PLAY LUCKY 7 FOR THIS EXCITING FREE GIFT!

THIS SURPRISE MYSTERY GIFT COULD BE YOURS FREE WHEN YOU PLAY

LUCKY 7!

DETACH AND MAIL CARD TODAY!

PLAY THE

LUCKY 7 SLOT MACHINE GAME!

Just scratch off the silver box with a coin. Then check below to see the gifts you get!

7 7 7

YES!

I have scratched off the silver box. Please send me all the gifts for which I qualify. I understand I am under no obligation to purchase any books, as explained on the back and on the opposite page.

235 SDL CH5L
(U-SIL-SE-07/98)

Name _____

PLEASE PRINT CLEARLY

Address _____ Apt.# _____

City _____ State _____ Zip _____

WORTH TWO FREE BOOKS PLUS A BONUS MYSTERY GIFT!

WORTH TWO FREE BOOKS!

WORTH ONE FREE BOOK!

TRY AGAIN!

The Silhouette Reader Service™ — Here's how it works

Accepting free books places you under no obligation to buy anything. You may keep the books and gift and return the shipping statement marked "cancel." If you do not cancel, about a month later we'll send you 6 additional novels, and bill you just $3.57 each, plus 25¢ delivery per book and applicable sales tax, if any.* That's the complete price — and compared to cover prices of $4.25 each — quite a bargain! You may cancel at any time, but if you choose to continue, every month we'll send you 6 more books, which you may either purchase at the discount price...or return to us and cancel your subscription.

*Terms and prices subject to change without notice. Sales tax applicable in N.Y.

If offer card is missing write to: Silhouette Reader Service, 3010 Walden Ave., P.O. Box 1867, Buffalo, NY 14240-1867

BUSINESS REPLY MAIL
FIRST-CLASS MAIL   PERMIT NO. 717   BUFFALO, NY

POSTAGE WILL BE PAID BY ADDRESSEE

SILHOUETTE READER SERVICE
3010 WALDEN AVE
PO BOX 1867
BUFFALO NY 14240-9952

NO POSTAGE
NECESSARY
IF MAILED
IN THE
UNITED STATES

"It was apparently easy enough to get them here."

"I'm sure Ali had to tell the food handler exactly what to do every step of the way."

"I take it he's eating somewhere else again?"

"That's right."

"And sleeping?"

"Wherever he chooses."

"I imagine your bodyguard does everything whenever and wherever he chooses."

"Pretty much."

"Was it difficult getting used to having someone watch your every move?" she asked curiously.

"That's always been a part of my life."

"Even in college?"

He smiled as if remembering something amusing. "Especially in college. I always had someone tailing me. Henry and I used to work out ways to lose them."

"Were you successful?"

"Sometimes. Especially when Henry was driving. There's nothing he wouldn't do to lose a tail."

"It must not have been Ali doing the tailing, then. You could never lose him."

Michael smiled and looked at his watch.

Jensen was instantly back on point. "Is it almost time? When are you meeting them?"

"In about twenty minutes."

"I want you to promise me that you'll tell me what they say as soon as you return."

"You might be asleep."

"Wake me."

"All right."

"Promise?"

"Promise."

They finished their sandwiches in silence, each preoccupied with their own thoughts.

Jensen opened her bag of chips and offered some to Michael.

"Thanks."

"I'm a bad influence."

"You're definitely an influence. Good, bad or indifferent. I haven't decided which kind yet."

He looked at his watch again. "I have to go."

"When will you be back."

"I don't know. But I'm taking Ali with me. I want your word that you won't leave the house."

Jensen didn't say anything.

"Your word, Jensen. I want you to promise me on your honor that you won't leave the house tonight."

She still didn't say anything.

Michael rose, but leaned over her and took her chin in his hand, raising her face so that she had no choice but to look at him. "Give me your word or I won't go."

He couldn't help worrying about her. She was impulsive and didn't always think through the consequences of her actions.

"All right," she said reluctantly. "You have my word."

"Don't let me down, Jensen." His eyes moved to her lips and stayed there for several seconds. "I'll talk to you later."

She watched as he left the room. The outer door closed a moment later and Jensen was alone.

She stayed on the couch for a while, but was restless. Rising, she paced from one end of the living room to the other, constantly looking at her watch.

One hour went by. Then two.

She opened the front door and stared outside, as if that would make Michael get back sooner.

She knew she should have followed him. She should never have made that promise.

Waiting was worse than any punishment.

Thoughts scattered through her mind.

What if something happened to Michael? Of course, there was Ali, but even Ali couldn't watch Michael's back all the time.

And who was watching Ali's back? The man was not superhuman, no matter what he thought.

No more promises. The next time there was any action, she was going to be right in the middle of it. No more of this sitting around the house business. No, sir.

What was that?

Jensen thought she heard something.

She listened very carefully, even stopping her breathing.

Nothing.

It was her imagination.

This was nerve-racking.

Hands suddenly came down on her shoulders. A scream tore into her throat.

Chapter Nine

Jensen spun around quickly, ready to fight, and found Michael standing there.

"You!" she nearly yelled at him. "What is this thing you have about sneaking up on me?"

"Sorry. I came in quietly because I thought you might be asleep. Once inside, there was no way to make myself known without frightening you."

"I still think you did it on purpose. Deep down in that kingly body lies a vicious prankster."

"Don't hold back, Jensen. Say what you really think."

"And how dare you—how *dare* you stay away so long without getting in touch with me to let me know you were all right." Her words came out in a rush. "Do you know the horrible thoughts I've been having? Can you imagine the torment I've been living, wondering if you and Ali were safe? Not to mention Henry. The very least you could have done, and I do mean the very least..."

Michael touched his fingers to her lips to silence her tirade. "Darling," he said softly, "we've found Henry. He's all right." Taking her by the hand, he led her to the couch.

Her eyes filled with sudden tears. They were doing that a lot lately. "Where is he?"

"Jail, I'm afraid."

"Jail? How can he be all right if he's in jail?"

"Believe me, it could have been worse. At least he's safe where he is."

"So you've seen him?"

"Yes. He has a window facing the street so I was able to see him and speak with him briefly."

"So all we have to do is bail him out and take him home. That's easy enough to do. I'll wire my bank for money first thing in the morning. It should only take..."

"There is no bail."

"No bail?" Jensen was having trouble following him. "But there has to be."

"You'd think so, but I'm afraid it's a little more complicated than that, Jensen."

"Why? What's he supposed to have done?"

"There are no charges."

"No charges? Then how can they hold him? Don't they have to let him go?"

"Jensen, this isn't the United States. People get put in jail and held for years without any charges being filed."

"We can't let that happen to Henry. We have to get him out, one way or another."

He pushed her hair away from her face. "I know. And we will. But not through normal channels."

"Meaning?"

"We're going to have to break him out."

Her lips parted softly. "Break him out?"

"That's right. It's the only way."

"How? When?"

Michael couldn't help the appreciative smile that lit his eyes. "You're game for anything, aren't you?"

"I don't know if 'game' is the word I'd use. I'm scared to death. I have been—except for a few moments—" she thought of the night in the tent and almost any time Michael was with her "—since I got here. I just know I need to do whatever it takes to get Henry home."

Michael got back on track. "Well, as I said, we'll have to break him out. The best time for that would be tomorrow when the guards are occupied with security at the auction."

Jensen rubbed her forehead. "Slave auction." She spoke in a whisper. "You mentioned that before. I can't imagine something like that in this day and age."

"I know. But it's gone on for a thousand years. Longer. It's how Adjani survives."

"Where do they get the people?"

"Some are abducted off the streets. Some are runaways in other countries, lured here by the promise of work, easy money or marriage to a rich man."

"And what happens to them when they're sold?"

"Whatever their owners want."

"And that's usually?"

"Labor or sex."

She leaned back against the couch.

"Tired?" he asked.

"Tired and disbelieving. The longer I'm here, the more I want to go home." She looked at Michael from the corner of her eye. "I don't suppose we could, say, crack the slave ring while we're here."

"No. But if it's any consolation to you, as soon as we get back to Sumaru, I'll see what I can do to undermine it."

"Thank you."

He reached out and touched her hair. "You've been through a lot in the past few days for someone who lives behind a computer, but you've held up remarkably well."

"I've made a conscious effort not to whine. The temptation at times, though, has been nearly over-whelming."

"What stopped you?"

"The thought of giving you and Ali the satisfaction."

Michael laughed out loud. "I see. I suppose I've been less than welcoming."

"You could say that."

"I'm sorry. I wasn't expecting you."

"Yes, you were. I called...."

"No, no," he said as he lifted her hair and let it run through his fingers. "I mean I wasn't expecting *you*."

"Is that good or bad?"

"Both. I was ready for Henry's little sister, and I imagined I'd like you because of that connection. I didn't expect to feel things for you independent of Henry."

"It's nice to know I'm not the only one."

As he trailed the back of his hand down her cheek, a corner of his mouth lifted.

"What?" she asked.

"I made a fuss over the fact that you touched me when we were in the desert, and I can't keep my hands off you."

"I'm not complaining."

"You should be."

"As you get to know me better—if you get to know me better—you'll find that I rarely do what I'm supposed to."

She looked into his eyes, her heart clearly visible in hers.

"Oh, Jensen, don't look at me like that. It tears at my heart and melts my hard-won resolve."

"I look at you the way I feel. I can't help it." She leaned toward him and touched her lips fleetingly to his, then leaned away when there was no response. "You could help a girl out a little," she said with an embarrassed smile.

"Jensen, you have to know that it would be foolish of both of us to take this any further."

"Don't you want me?"

Michael looked away as he shook his head.

"Is that a yes or a no?"

He returned his gaze to Jensen. "Want you?" His

voice was nearly hoarse with passion. "I ache with wanting. It invades every cell of my body."

"I'm sensing a but."

His eyes moved over her lovely face. "But I've learned in life that you can't always have what you want."

"I'm here, Michael. And I want you, too."

He trailed the backs of his fingers down her cheek again. "Anything more than friendship between the two of us impossible."

"Why?"

"I'm to be married, Jensen."

"To a woman you don't love."

"That doesn't make it any less true."

"You're not married yet."

"Let's say we make love tonight. Let's say we allow ourselves to feel everything we're destined to feel if that happens. What becomes of us when I do get married?"

"I don't want to think that far ahead."

"Then I have to, for both of us."

"Don't think," she said as she cupped his face in her hands and drew his mouth to hers. "Just don't think."

Michael responded despite himself, his body pressing hers into the couch as she pulled him down with her. She moved her hands over his shoulders and down his back to his hips, pressing him more tightly against her.

Michael groaned and raised his head so that he could gaze into her luminous eyes. "This is reckless."

"I don't care."

He kissed the corners of her mouth, teasing her, then kissing her deeply, as though it came from his soul.

He pushed himself off of her and stood up. Jensen looked at him, wondering what he was doing.

He suddenly scooped her into his arms, carried her to his room and closed the door with his foot.

Setting her gently on her feet, Michael slowly undressed her, undoing her blouse one button at a time, his warm hands between her breasts, then sliding those hands over her shoulders, under the fabric and slipping it down her arms.

It fell to the floor.

Michael looked at her for a long moment, drinking in her beauty, then bent his head and kissed first one breast then the other, taking his time, using his tongue to stiffen her nipples then gently sucking.

Jensen closed her eyes and arched her back as his mouth moved down her stomach. With sure hands, he unzipped her skirt and it fell in a soft fabric cloud around her feet.

Again he lifted her in his arms and carried her to the bed, moving aside the mosquito netting and laying her in the middle. As he straightened away from Jensen, his eyes swept over her body. He slowly unbuttoned and took off his own shirt.

Climbing into the bed beside Jensen, he pulled her into his arms and held her, savoring her closeness. "God help us," he whispered against her lips.

There was a knock on the door.

Michael raised his head. "Yes?"

"May I come in?" asked Ali.

"Not now," said Michael.

"We need to discuss what we're going to do tomorrow."

"I know," said Michael. "We'll talk in the morning."

"Yes, Your Highness."

When he'd gone, Michael rolled with a groan onto his back, his hand over his forehead.

Jensen turned onto her stomach and kissed his shoulder. "Don't turn away from me."

"We can't do this."

"I have to tell you," said Jensen, "that I'm usually the most guilt-ridden person on the planet, but I feel absolutely no guilt about the two of us making love."

"But I do."

"My heroines would never let you off this easily."

"Oh? What would they do?"

Jensen rested her cheek on his shoulder.

"Do you really want to know?"

"I wouldn't have asked if I didn't."

Jensen snuggled against him more deeply. "Well, first she'd kiss you," said Jensen, "long and deep. And while she was kissing you, she'd slowly move her hand over your chest and abdomen, trailing her fingertips over your increasingly sensitive skin. Perhaps she'd toy with your nipples, kissing them, teasing them.

"She'd move her hand along the outside of your thigh, then up between your legs and lightly caress you. You'd moan softly, wanting to move away, but unable to resist the pleasure.''

"Jensen," said Michael.

But she wasn't about to stop. "Then her fingertips would move over your erect staff, finding the most sensitive spot and lightly—almost like the touch of a butterfly's wings—touch you, and then stop. Touch you and then stop. Then she would grasp you completely and slowly begin to move her hand up and down, still gently, making sure her fingertips are flitting over the most sensitive part.''

Michael groaned out loud.

"When she felt you were ready, she would climb on top of you. Ever so slowly, she would let you enter her an inch at a time until you filled her completely.

"You would try to move, but she would force you to lie still so she could feel you growing even more inside her, larger and larger until she could barely stand it herself.

"She would slowly raise herself over you and then lower herself until you were out of control. You would flip her onto her back and begin thrusting inside her, bringing her with you, harder and faster until the two of you explode together in complete release.''

Michael was absolutely silent.

"Still with me?" she asked, pleased with herself, knowing exactly what she'd done to him.

"Oh, yes." He turned his head to look at her. "This is what you write?"

"Pretty much.''

He let out a long breath.

"It got to you, didn't it?"

"No comment."

"I'm right here," she whispered against his ear. "And I'm not a book. I'm flesh and blood. All you have to do is reach out and touch me, Michael."

She moved her body against his.

His arm gripped her more tightly. "Don't move," he said sharply. "Just stay statue still."

Jensen did.

"I'm going to have to start reading your books."

"More men should. They'd learn a lot about women."

"The thing is, I don't want any other men reading your books."

She kissed him behind the ear.

Michael suddenly rose from the bed. "You sleep in here tonight. I'll go in the other room."

Jensen rolled onto her back and sighed. "My first seduction and it's a complete bust."

Michael walked back to the bed as naked as the day he was born, completely unselfconscious about either his state of nakedness or arousal. He leaned over Jensen and kissed her long and hard. "Believe me, you were more successful than you'll ever know."

"But you're leaving the room."

"Because if I don't, I won't be responsible for my actions. I want you so badly I hurt."

"Then take me. I want you to."

"If we make love, I'll never be able to let you

go. Can you understand that? And I must let you go.''

Jensen reached up and cupped his face in her hand. ''You are the most honorable of men, and it makes me love you all the more.''

''I don't want to be the cause of any pain for you.''

''I know,'' she said softly. ''I know.''

He kissed her again. ''Good night.''

''Night.''

''Michael?''

He turned back.

''If I promise to be good, will you just stay with me and hold me?''

''It's too difficult.''

''I won't do anything or say anything to tempt you. Honest. I just want to be with you any way I can. This is our last chance. Once Henry is safe tomorrow, we'll be going our separate ways.''

Still Michael hesitated.

''Please.''

Against his better judgment, Michael climbed back into the bed and lay on his back. Jensen put her head on his shoulder, but was careful to keep her hand on his chest.

And she lay very still.

Michael rubbed his hand up and down the soft skin of her bare arm and held her close.

Once again, while he lay wide-awake, Jensen was able to sleep. He could feel her deep, even breaths.

He had never known it was possible to want a woman as much as he wanted her.

To love the way he loved her.

She touched something inside him that no one else ever had. Other women in his life faded into insignificance.

Only Jensen was real.

He was still awake when the sun came up.

Jensen, her head still on his shoulder, her legs entwined with his, her hand on his taut stomach, stirred.

Michael touched his lips to her hair. He didn't want to give her up. Not now. Not ever.

He held her more tightly.

And as he held her more tightly, Jensen slowly awoke to the awareness that she was safely wrapped in Michael's arms. It was no dream this time. A sleepy smile curved her mouth as she kissed his shoulder and looked up at him. "Good morning."

He ran his strong hand down her arm. His eyes were warm and loving—and sad—as he pulled her body level with his so that her head lay on the pillow facing him. "I should have known you'd be beautiful first thing in the morning."

There was a knock. It was Ali. He spoke through the door in Arabic and Michael answered him. Then, with his body raised slightly over Jensen, he gazed down at her, knowing he would remember the way she looked at that moment, with her golden hair spilling over the pillow and her eyes full of love, for the rest of his life. "It's time to go."

Jensen raised her hand to his face one more time then, with a sigh, rose from the bed, picked up her clothes from the floor and went to her own bedroom through their connecting bathroom.

She heard Michael take a quick shower with the limited water. When he'd finished, Jensen did the same, washing her hair with just a little shampoo and rinsing it.

The first thing she was going to do when she got back to Wisconsin was take a long, long shower.

When she got back to her bedroom, Michael knocked on her door.

Still wrapped in her towel, she opened it. Ali was hovering in the background.

"I want you to dress differently today," said Michael. "We need you as a distraction for the guard."

"By differently, you mean like a woman?"

"A sexy woman."

"But all I brought other than the skirt from last night are khaki shorts and a long-sleeved shirt."

"Do the best you can. And then put the robe on over it. And the headdress."

"All right."

Jensen pulled out the clothes and stared at them. What on earth could she do with such basically drab clothes?

She put on the shorts first. They reached midthigh and were cuffed. Jensen looked at herself in the mirror and wrinkled her nose. Even a man who'd been alone in the desert for two months wouldn't give her a second look.

She began rolling up the legs a cuff length at a time until they were as short as she could possibly get them.

Much better. She had good legs. Long and still somewhat tanned looking from the stain.

Next she put on the blouse.

Blah.

She rolled up the sleeves so that they came to the middle of her upper arms.

It didn't work.

Opening the door, she poked her head around it. "Michael, can you find me a pair of scissors?"

"Sure. Just a minute."

She heard him rattling around the kitchen. A moment later he returned with a nice big pair.

"Thank you."

"What are you doing?"

"You'll see."

Closing the door, she took off the blouse and carefully cut off both sleeves about half an inch below the shoulder seam so that she could tuck the excess material back into the blouse without the frayed ends being visible.

This time when she tried it on, it worked.

Yesterday she hadn't worn a bra. It was just too hot. But today, she pulled a black lace, front fastening one out of her backpack—just one of those necessities one didn't travel without—and put it on. It wasn't a push-up bra, however, and while it looked nice, and even somewhat sexy, it wasn't eye-popping.

Walking into the bathroom, she unrolled several feet of toilet tissue from the roll and stuffed it under one of her breasts as she looked in the mirror.

"Perfect," she said aloud, with a smile at the sudden amount of cleavage that made an appearance.

Then she did the same with the other side.

Picture-perfect.

Back in her room, she put on the blouse and left the entire thing unbuttoned so that her cleavage was prominently displayed and tied the two front ends of the blouse in a square knot just below her breasts, leaving her midriff bare.

And it was a good-looking midriff.

"Thank you, Jesse," she said, with a whispered appreciative nod to the personal trainer who worked her so hard three days a week in the gym back home.

Michael knocked on her door. "Are you ready to go?"

"One more minute." Grabbing the robe, she slipped it over her head and let it hang loosely, then wound her hair around her head, fastening it with a single clip, and put the headdress on.

Now, she was ready.

The question was, was that guard ready for her.

Chapter Ten

After a final critical look in the mirror, Jensen grabbed her backpack and left her room. Michael and Ali were both impatiently waiting for her in the living room.

"You still haven't told me what we're going to do," she said as Michael took the backpack and tossed it onto the couch. "I mean, it would be helpful if I knew the plan."

"You don't need to take this. We'll be back to pick it up along with our other things," he said as he walked ahead of her, out the front door to the car.

Ali climbed into the second car.

"The auction is happening even as we speak and will continue throughout the day. Ali double-checked this morning and found that there is only one guard in the jail. The main door into the building faces a narrow alley. We're going to park one car at one end of the alley and disable it. You'll go into the jail, get the jailer and have him help you try to start the car. I'll be parked at the other end of the alley. While you keep the guard turned away from the jail, I'll go in and get Henry and take him back to the house. After we leave, Ali will happen by, fix the car and then you'll drive a block away where you'll pick up Ali and the two of you will meet us at the house. When night falls, we'll leave the city."

"Sounds simple enough."

"Almost too simple."

"Question: Won't they set up roadblocks to find Henry?"

A corner of Michael's mouth lifted. "Contrary to what Henry thinks, he isn't that important to them. If he were, they'd never leave him in that ancient jail with one guard. I still haven't figured out why they arrested him in the first place. It's not as though no one has ever done a story on the slave market before."

"Perhaps he came up with some new and incriminating information that could put an end to the misery."

Michael shook his head. "I don't think so. Something else is going on here. I don't know what yet, but before this business is finished, I'll find out."

"What makes you think all isn't as it seems?"

"Gut instinct. That's why I'm a little uneasy

about getting Henry out of jail. It's as though the whole thing were set up for us.''

''That's what you meant when you said it was too easy.''

Michael nodded.

Jensen sighed. ''Great. You couldn't leave it alone. I was just fine and now I'm nervous.''

''Good. That means you'll be careful.''

Jensen looked at Michael's profile. ''Anything else I should know going into this?''

''I can guarantee you that the guard will speak little if any English, but I want you to flirt up a storm with him anyway. Make him focus on you completely and keep his back to the jail. Just act like a normal woman in distress.''

''Piece of cake.''

''I know,'' said Michael grimly as he backed the car out of the driveway and headed into town.

Jensen turned in her seat to make sure Ali was behind them.

He was. As always.

This time she found it comforting.

The streets didn't seem as crowded as they had the day before. People were no doubt at the auction. No one paid any attention to them as they drove past.

They took a circuitous route through the grungy town and came back the other way so that they were parked pointing in the direction of the house.

''Henry's in there,'' said Michael, inclining his head toward the building they were in front of.

Jensen saw a small stone one-story building that

couldn't have held more than three cells. It looked like something out of the Wild West. Or at least a television show about the Wild West.

"You can't be serious," said Jensen. "That's it? That's all they have for all of the criminals in the whole city?"

"It takes a lot to get jailed in Adjani."

"And somehow Henry managed to qualify. He should be given an award."

"Henry somehow ticked off the wrong people," said Michael as he looked at his watch. "He's lucky he was jailed and not killed. Are you ready?"

She took off the headdress and unpinned her hair, then took off the robe.

Ali walked up to the car and spoke to Michael in Arabic as Jensen tossed her things into the back seat. Then he walked away from them, down the street.

"What did he say?"

"There's still only one jailer, as before."

Michael looked her up and down and shook his head. "You're beautiful."

"And cheap."

"No. Just beautiful. The jailer is going to think he died and went to heaven."

Jensen took a deep breath as Michael looked down the street to see if anyone was coming.

"Frightened?" he asked.

"Oh, yes."

"I'm sorry you have to do this."

"It's all right. It's for Henry. And he's going to owe me big time for the rest of his life. That alone makes it worthwhile."

Michael looked in the rearview mirror. "Ali has the hood up. He's disconnected a small wire to disable the engine. Chances are good that the guard is going to be more interested in you than the engine. Keep it that way."

"No problem."

"Good luck. And don't take any chances with yourself. I want to get Henry, but I don't want to lose you in the process."

"I'll be careful."

"Give me just two minutes to get around to the other side of the alley."

Jensen got out of Michael's car and walked back to the other one, looking under the hood as she heard Michael drive off. When two minutes had passed, she walked through the alley to the door of the jail. She could see the front of Michael's car at the other end.

It was time.

Taking a deep breath, she pulled back her shoulders, opened the door and walked inside.

It was quite a bit darker inside than out and it took a moment for her eyes to adjust to the dimness. When they did, she saw a small man in uniform sitting behind a desk, his legs propped up, not looking particularly busy.

He looked at Jensen in such complete disbelief at what she was wearing—and not wearing—that it would have been comical if it weren't so deadly serious.

He nearly fell out of his chair as he tried to rise too quickly and lost his balance.

Jensen bit her lip in an effort not to smile. Any woman who said she didn't feel a certain surge of power at being able to immobilize a man with her body wasn't being completely honest. She could almost pinpoint the moment when the man stopped thinking with his brain.

He hurried around his desk, his face beaming, and asked her a question in Arabic.

"Do you speak English?" she asked.

He frowned.

"English? American?"

"American?" he repeated as he eyed her up and down.

"I guess not. Well," she continued as though he did, "perhaps you can help me anyway." She pointed in the direction of the street. "I need help. My car has broken down."

He raised his hands as if in supplication and shrugged as he spoke in Arabic.

Jensen signaled him with her finger to follow her outside and started walking.

The guard followed, as she knew he would.

Once in the alley, she pointed in the direction of the street and kept walking.

When they got to the end of the alley, she pointed once again at the car. As soon as he saw the hood propped up, communication was complete. Leaning over the engine, he jabbered away at her as he poked here and there.

Jensen didn't have a very good view of the alley from the front of the car, so she moved around behind the guard and spotted Michael just as he entered the jail.

She quickly went back to the hood, leaned over the engine to give the guard a better view, and smiled at him.

He signaled her to try to start the car.

Jensen climbed inside, pushed in the clutch and turned the key in the ignition. The Hummer sounded as though it wanted to start. It really seemed to make a hopeful effort, but whined to a stop.

The guard fiddled with the wiring a little more, then made the starting motion again.

She complied.

The car made the same noise.

Jensen got out of the car and leaned over the engine again. Poor guy. If only he knew she was more tissue than flesh in the area that interested him the most.

She tried to be helpful, pointing first at one part of the engine and then another—making sure he didn't give up too quickly.

She indicated the radiator coolant.

He shook his head.

Then she pointed at the battery.

He shook his head again.

Straightening, she walked around behind him again and glanced down the alley. Michael was there with Henry in tow and they were nearly halfway to the car.

Jensen was so happy to see her brother alive and well that she wanted to run to him, but confined herself to a secret smile and went back to the engine to watch the guard while he fiddled.

She was growing a little afraid that he might break the car for real because he was doing some serious poking around.

Finally she spotted Ali walking toward them. He spoke to the guard and the two men both leaned under the hood. Ali pointed to the wire he'd loosened earlier. The guard nodded and reattached it, then signaled Jensen to try the engine again.

This time, of course, the car started perfectly and the guard felt like a hero. Surely no one was more surprised than he at his good luck in finding just the right wire.

The guard beamed at her, proud of being her rescuer, and she smiled warmly back.

As Ali went on his way down the street, Jensen tried to drive off, but the guard didn't want her to leave. She couldn't understand the language, but it was clear enough that she was being invited back to the jail for some tea.

Jensen smilingly tapped the face of her watch as if to say that she had no time.

He looked at her pleadingly.

Jensen shrugged her shoulders sympathetically and pointed at her watch again, managing to appear regretful, then put the car into gear and headed down the street.

The guard watched her for a few moments then, heaving a great sigh, headed back toward the jail.

Jensen turned the corner and saw Ali waiting for

her. As she stopped the car, Ali signaled to her to get out so he could drive.

"Chauvinist," she said, only half joking as she walked around the car.

A man shouted.

Both Jensen and Ali looked up, suddenly alert.

For a single, horrified moment, Jensen thought it was the guard chasing them down. But then she saw four men walking toward her. She recognized the one in the lead instantly as the man in the desert who had tried to buy her from Michael.

And he was looking straight at her.

"Ali," she said uncertainly. "What do we do?"

He looked in the direction she was looking, but by that time it was too late. The men were upon them. Before Ali could react, he was hit from behind by one of the men who had circled around behind him and went down, unconscious.

Jensen ran to help him, but the man from the desert grabbed her around the waist and tossed her over his shoulder as though she were nothing more than a rag doll.

Jensen wasn't about to go easily. She slammed her foot hard into his groin, but he just kept walking.

She grabbed his headdress and pulled it off, then grabbed a handful of his greasy hair and yanked on it as hard as she could.

The man suddenly stopped walking, set her on the ground and slugged her.

Jensen felt a blinding pain in her head, absolute disbelief that she'd been hit—and then nothing.

* * *

Michael was nervously pacing, repeatedly checking for Ali's car. "They should have been back by now," he said.

Henry, who looked like a male version of his sister with his blond hair and green eyes, agreed. "Maybe we should go back and look for them."

"Not you. You stay here."

Henry was firm. "No. This is my baby sister we're talking about. If Jen's in trouble because of me, then I need to get her out."

Michael put his hand on his friend's shoulder. "Let me go on my own just to see what's going on. You can't go showing your face in town. If you get caught, you won't be able to help anybody, much less Jensen. If I find out that she needs us, I'll come back for you."

Michael climbed into the car and was backing out of the driveway when Ali pulled up beside him with a squeal of brakes.

The first thing Michael noticed was that Jensen wasn't in the car. He physically felt his heart sink. "What happened?" he all but yelled as he jumped out of the car.

Ali, his head bloodied, walked over to him. "She was taken by the nomad."

"How did it happen?"

"He and some of his men came down the street at the same time your Jensen was picking me up. They caught us both by surprise, knocked me out and grabbed her."

"Did you see anything? Do you even know what

direction they went in?'' asked Michael as he dragged his fingers through his hair.

''No.''

''She could be anywhere,'' he said hoarsely.

Henry came flying out of the house. ''What's going on?''

''She's gone,'' said Michael.

''Gone?''

''Kidnapped.''

''By whom? Why?''

''A nomad. His name is Habib. We came across him in the desert only a couple of days ago. He tried to buy Jensen from me.''

''Oh, my God. What do we do?''

Michael pulled himself together. He had to. ''Okay. He probably stayed in town. If he were to head for the desert, we'd stand a good chance of finding him and he knows that. In town, our chances are a lot slimmer.''

''What do you suppose he wants with her?''

Michael looked at Henry, but didn't say anything.

Henry's jaw tightened. ''If he so much as lays a finger on her, so help me, I'll kill the jerk.''

''We have to be realistic. Habib has taken Jensen because he wants her, and he may well—he may harm her. And when he's finished, he'll probably try to sell her. She'll bring him a very good price on the open market.''

''But the slave auction is going on today. Surely he won't want to give her up so quickly?''

''Of course not. But there are private buyers who wait a lifetime for a prize like your sister. All he has to do is shop her around, and he can do that at his leisure."

Henry was at a loss. He'd been following the slave market story long enough to know what happened to the women who got caught in the net. "What are we going to do, Michael? This can't happen to my sister. She'll never survive it."

Michael felt physically ill, but he still managed to put a comforting hand on Henry's shoulder. "The first thing I'm going to do is send out search planes. This guy travels on horseback. As I said, I don't think he went into the desert, but if he did, he won't get far."

"And if he's in town?"

"This requires a little more delicacy. I can't do anything that will be perceived by Sheik Ahmed as aggression against him or his rule. He has a quick temper and loves to fight. And, frankly, he's wanted to get his hands on my country ever since he took over his father's throne. He must have no excuse to retaliate against anything I do."

"Which leaves us where?" asked Henry.

"I'm going to bring in plainclothesmen to mingle with the general population to ask questions and quietly search for Jensen."

"You could be wrong about Habib's intention of keeping her for himself for a while. What if he's selling her even as we're standing here?" Henry asked.

"I really don't think he will. He wants Jensen for himself."

"But how can you know that with any certainty?"

Michael met Henry's eyes. "I saw the way he looked at her when we were in the desert."

Henry's eyes grew steely. "So what do we do first?"

Michael turned to Ali. "Are you all right, my friend? Your head looks as though it needs to be tended."

"I'm fine. There's no time to waste on me. We must find your Jensen."

"Yes," agreed Michael. "And quickly. The first thing I need you to do is get Henry a robe and headdress so he's less conspicuous."

"It will be done," said Ali. Then he turned to Henry. "I swear to you on my life that I will find your sister and return her safely to you. She was entrusted to my care and I let her down. The nomad Habib will regret this day's work."

Ali had a look in his eye that made Henry grateful they were on the same side. "Thank you."

Michael nodded. "All right. I'm going to leave now and begin checking the slave auction. You wait here for your clothes and then stay with Ali."

"But I thought you said she wouldn't be there," said Henry.

"We have to start somewhere. If there's even a small chance she's at the auction, we can't afford to overlook it."

It was the jostling that caused Jensen to regain consciousness. That, and the pain in her jaw.

She slowly opened her eyes and saw steps.

Steps?

She had been tossed over someone's shoulder, her hands and feet bound and a blanket thrown over her. Jensen wriggled, trying to set herself free.

A hand crashed down on her rear end, painfully hard. Jensen cried out.

She heard a door being kicked open. She was carried into a room and thrown carelessly onto a bed.

The man who had slugged Jensen now stood before her, arms akimbo as he looked down at her. He snapped his fingers at someone, but never took his eyes from her.

A moment later a man handed him a bottle. He grabbed her by the hair.

Jensen screamed. As soon as she opened her mouth, he poured in the liquid from the bottle. Jensen choked on it, swallowing some, spitting out what she could back into the man's face.

He set the bottle down and, still grasping her hair, crashed his hand into her face again. It didn't knock her out this time, but it hurt. The nomad pushed her back on the bed and leered down at her. He said something in Arabic that made another man in the room laugh. Then he leaned over Jensen and pinched her nose until she had to open her mouth for air, then poured more of the liquid into her.

When he'd finished, he stuffed a rag into her mouth, then just stood there watching as the drug slowly and completely drained the fight from her helpless body.

Jensen fought to stay awake. She was terrified of losing what little control she had.

And she wanted to know exactly what was happening to her at all times. But the drug was too strong for her. Warm, furious tears ran from the corners of her eyes into her hair. Tears of rage and frustration and helplessness.

Her eyelids fluttered shut.

Michael, she screamed silently. Where are you?

Then everything went black.

Chapter Eleven

Michael went straight to the seedy restaurant he'd stopped at the night before and used the phone in the back to call his minister of defense. He had a satellite phone, but didn't want the call to be picked up or monitored in any way.

"We have a problem."

"Your Highness?"

"I'm calling from Adjani. An American woman who was with me was kidnapped this morning. I want airplanes dispatched to search the desert near here."

"To look for?"

"Any nomadic activity in the areas of Adjani within a one-hundred-miles radius."

"That means flying in air space that doesn't belong to us. We need the permission of the sheik of Adjani.''

"Then get it. Just don't tell him the reason. This is strictly a need to know operation.''

"Yes, sir.''

"I also want land vehicles sent to blanket the area with nonuniformed soldiers and a dozen men sent to Adjani to coordinate a complete search of the city.''

"We're getting into extremely dangerous and touchy territory, Your Highness. Perhaps, since the woman is an American, we should let the Americans handle it on their own and not put ourselves in the way of so much overt risk.''

"No. Jensen O'Hara was and remains my responsibility. I, whether it's personally or by the efforts of my country, will be the one who finds her. Do you understand?''

"Yes, of course. But I must reemphasize that this should be done through proper channels with authorities in Adjani. Otherwise our movements could be considered a declaration of war.''

"Ahmed knows me better than that.''

"But his ministers don't. You're new to this job. They don't have your measure yet.''

"I don't want police or any other local law enforcement here informed. I'm very firm on that point.''

"Including the sheik?''

"No. He should be made aware that she's missing, but not of our search.''

"You're aware that he will speak only with you.

I, as your minster of defense, would not be considered important enough to pass information to him directly."

"Protocol."

"Yes, sir."

"If he's in the city, set up a meeting for me with him as soon as possible."

"Of course."

"I just hate the waste of time. We need to find Jensen and we need to find her now."

"Are you certain she's still in the vicinity?"

"She was taken less than an hour ago. The only airfield around here belongs to the sheik. She's either in the city or just outside it with the nomad Habib. So yes, I'm sure she's in the vicinity. I just need to precisely pinpoint where."

"Yes, sir."

"I don't want anyone who isn't handpicked by you or me to know about the fact that Jensen is missing or the steps we're taking to find her. Do you understand?"

"Yes, sir."

"And I want men sent into the city to search for her now, not after my meeting with Ahmed. Surely even Ahmed wouldn't consider looking for a kidnapped woman an act of aggression. Have them helicoptered to our country's border and then driven the rest of the way to avoid an obvious entry into the city."

"It will be done just as you ask."

"I'll call you back regarding my meeting with Ahmed as soon as it's occurred. Never mind making an appointment. I'm here. I'll just show up on his doorstep. He won't turn me away.''

''Your Highness, there's one other matter. The young man named Yusef who first made us aware of Miss O'Hara's plight a few days ago returned today claiming he had uncovered more information regarding her brother's disappearance.''

''That's old news. Send the boy home. We've already recovered Henry.''

''He seems to believe that the imprisonment of your friend was not what it appeared to be on the surface.''

''Then what was it?''

''He refuses to speak with anyone but you. He says you're the only one he trusts. And that it's a matter of life and death.''

Michael hesitated. He didn't like dragging a boy into this, but he needed all the help he could get. ''Find him and have him brought here to me.''

''It will be done.''

''Thank you.''

When he'd hung up the phone, Michael just stood there completely still. He was sick at the thought of what might be happening to Jensen at that moment.

And furious at his helplessness to stop it.

''I'll find you, Jensen O'Hara,'' he whispered. ''Wherever you are—however long it takes—I'll find you. And I'll make whoever did this to you pay.''

The marketplace was on the outskirts of the town, in the opposite direction of the house he'd rented.

The Hummer barely made it through the narrow maze of streets. But suddenly everything opened up to a large plaza teeming with men in robes and expensive suits, their headdresses a bobbing sea of color.

Michael found a spot to park, put on sunglasses to cover his blue eyes and joined the crowd of robed and suited buyers. It took some maneuvering, but he worked his way through the mass of men to the stage where a man was shouting about the fine physical qualities to be found in the young woman standing passively beside him, her arms bound behind her back, her face half-hidden by a shock of red hair.

He watched as the bidding began, feeing ill, but helpless to stop what was happening. He'd known about this since childhood, but it had never really affected him. It was accepted and rarely discussed.

There was some lively bidding for the woman. In the end, she went to an older man for a moderate price and was led off the stage to be paid for and picked up by her new owner.

While another woman—this one clearly drugged—was being brought up, Michael got closer to the stage and signaled to the auctioneer that he wanted to talk to him.

The man leaned down.

"I'm looking for someone very specific," Michael said. "About so high—" he motioned with his hand "—long blond hair, green eyes, very beautiful. Have you seen anyone like that today?"

"A couple."

"Have they already been sold?"

"No. We save those for last. They keep our bidders around. We sell more."

"I want to see them."

"No, no. We never allow potential bidders any previews of the merchandise."

Michael looked around and discreetly handed him the equivalent of a hundred dollars.

The auctioneer looked over Michael's head to see if anyone was watching. "Double it, my friend, and you can tell the guards at the gate I said to let you in."

Michael handed him another hundred. "And if I find the woman I want, there will be more."

He smiled, flashing tobacco-yellowed teeth. "Help yourself," he said with a wave.

Pushing his way through the crowd, Michael was stopped by gun-toting guards. They looked toward the auctioneer and he signaled that Michael was to be allowed through.

Behind the scenes, things were remarkably quiet. The victims were mostly women, but there were some men. Some were seated; some standing. Guards stood at the corners, arms in evidence, watching over their charges.

Woman by woman, Michael made his way through the captives, examining every blank face, fully aware that Jensen's hair could have been cut or dyed.

And with every strange face, there was disappointment. And then he said a little prayer that the next one would be her and moved on.

He was nearly at the end when he saw her about

ten feet away. It was just the back of her head, but he would have known that long, blond hair anywhere. Thank God. His entire body flooded with relief. He strode straight toward her and touched her shoulder. "Jensen, I'm here."

At the touch of his hand, the woman turned her head and looked up at him with dead blue eyes.

It wasn't Jensen.

Michael's hand fell to his side. "Excuse me. I thought you were someone else."

She looked away, expressionless, without saying anything.

But it could have been his Jensen. She could have been put on the market like a piece of meat, the way the others were.

His father may have had good reason not to interfere with this, but he'd never seen it firsthand. Finding Jensen was Michael's first order of business.

His second was going to be shutting this operation down. And if it took an act of war against Sheik Ahmed to do it, then so be it.

Jensen slowly opened her eyes. They felt so heavy, it almost took more effort than she could summon.

She closed them again.

"Jensen?" said a man's voice softly. "Jensen O'Hara? It's time for you to wake up."

She opened her eyes again. But open and focused were two entirely different things. A man sat in a chair beside the bed. At least she thought it was a man. Mostly he was a blur.

"Michael?" she asked.

"I'm afraid it's not."

As soon as Jensen heard the voice again, she knew it wasn't Michael. "Who are you?"

"Think of me as a fan."

"A fan?"

"Of your books."

"You read romance novels?" Even in her drugged state, she was surprised. A man admitting to reading romance novels? It was completely unheard-of.

"I read yours. I have ever since we met at an ambassador's ball a year ago."

Jensen stared hard, but her eyes just wouldn't focus properly. "I don't remember..."

"You were there with your brother. We danced."

"I danced with a lot of people that night. It was a large party."

"Yes, you did."

Jensen let out an exhausted sigh. "Why am I here? What do you want with me?"

"I'm surprised with all that imagination of yours that you haven't figured it out."

"I guess I'm a little slow when I've been knocked unconscious and drugged. Which, incidentally, is no way to win a woman's heart, if that's your intention."

As he sat beside her on the bed, Jensen felt the mattress sink under his weight. "I'm sorry about Habib hitting you," he said as he gently touched her bruised cheek. "He overstepped his bounds. But you have to admit you were being difficult. He was simply doing his job in bringing you here to my palace.''

She sharply jerked her head away from his fingers. ''Don't you touch me.''

''I can touch you when I wish, wherever I wish, Miss O'Hara. You belong to me now.''

Her vision was getting better all the time, but still wasn't completely clear. ''What kind of ridiculous remark is that? You can't own another human being.''

''You think not?'' he asked calmly.

''I know it.''

''But you're here, aren't you?''

''Not voluntarily.''

''Volunteerism isn't required for ownership. I should think that very few people would volunteer for that, unless they're in love. Nevertheless, the fact remains that I possess you. I paid the nomad good money to bring you here. Good enough to keep him in comfort for the rest of his life as long as he keeps his mouth shut. You are in my palace and you will not leave here unless and until I say you can.''

''You may have made me a prisoner,'' Jensen said, ''but I don't belong to you.''

''You Americans think that because you say it, that makes it so.'' He touched her face again. ''So naive. So trusting. I think you'll soon come to understand that you do indeed belong to me. In every intimate sense of the word. At least, you soon will.''

''Meaning what? That you're going to rape me?'' Her eyes were focusing now, on a very handsome man, perhaps thirty, with warm brown eyes and a dark beard. "I remember you now," she said. "You're the man at the hotel who bumped into me. And at that dance, you stood off to the side and watched me all evening. You're Sheik Ahmed."

"Yes, I am. And not all evening."

"We danced once," said Jensen. "The next day you sent me an extravagant diamond-and-emerald necklace."

"Which you returned to me by messenger later in the morning with a politely impersonal note."

"I thought that would be the end of it."

"Oh, no. That only whet my appetite for you."

"But not mine for you."

"Circumstances have a way of changing feelings. You'll be ready for me when I come to you tonight."

"Not a chance."

"Oh, I think there's a very good chance."

"So you believe that by forcing me to give you my body, you'll win my heart?"

"I care nothing for your heart. There are dozens of women who willingly bestow theirs upon me."

"Without my heart, you can never truly own me."

"I think we have different definitions for the word 'own.'"

Jensen couldn't believe this was happening. It was like something out of a nightmare. Any minute she was going to wake up, safe in Michael's arms.

The man stroked her long hair. "You're so beautiful. From the moment I first saw you at that ball, I knew I had to have you."

"Are you saying that you've been planning this kidnapping for more than a year?"

"Every detail." He smiled at her. "You're very predictable, Jensen. I knew if you believed your brother was missing, you'd come here to find him."

"I'm not following you."

"First I lured Henry to the Middle East and then I lured him to Adjani, where I had him arrested."

It was beginning to fall into place. "You're the one who made the phone call to my home...."

"Well, I had someone make it. Then I left little clues for you to follow."

"You sent the guide to the hotel? The one who claimed he'd been sent by the embassy."

"That's right."

"And you had him dump me in the desert."

"Yes. And Habib was supposed to fetch you for me. What I didn't count on was your being rescued by someone else. And particularly not by the sheik of the neighboring country. I must admit that made things a bit awkward."

"So this whole exercise has been nothing more than a plot to get me here?"

"Exactly."

"Did it ever occur to you to simply introduce yourself?"

"But we were introduced and you clearly weren't interested. You returned my necklace."

"Women can't accept gifts of that extravagance from strangers. It just isn't done."

"Other women have."

"Well, I don't."

"Perhaps you should have. Then we could have avoided all of this. Although I have to admit that the hunt for you has been surprisingly pleasant. Plotting what to do and how you'd react. Almost like a chess game, really."

"You should have left it at that."

"Oh, no. I couldn't allow someone else to get near you. I wanted you then and I want you now."

"You want me for what?" Jensen asked.

"To share my bed."

"Then it will have to be rape because I'll certainly never willingly come to you."

His mouth straightened into a tight line. "Am I so repugnant to you? I assure you, there are many women who would be honored."

"So you mentioned earlier. Why not ask one of them to sleep with you?"

"But you're the one I want."

"Why? Why me?"

"Everything I thought about you the night we met, I discovered to be true when I read your books. You are the kind of woman I can love. The kind I want to love me."

"What you read is fiction."

He shook his head. "Don't tell me those aren't your emotions you're writing about."

"Some of them are, of course."

He leaned forward and looked into her eyes. "I know the kind of man you want...the kind of man you can love. I can be that man for you, Jensen."

Jensen looked directly back at him. "No, you can't. The kind of man I can love already has the qualities you saw in the books. He doesn't have to develop them. I want a man who already is intelligent, honorable, loving and honest, not one who has to pretend.''

''You sound as though you've already found him.''

''I have.''

''Who is he?''

''It doesn't matter.''

''I want to know.''

Jensen just glared at him. ''I'm going to be missed. People will come looking for me.''

''Like your brother? He won't know where to start. Or Michael Hassan? He would never suspect me of kidnapping you. We grew up together, you know, until he went to the United States to school. You might even say that we're friends.''

''Michael would never be friends with someone like you.''

''He would if circumstances dictated it.''

''What circumstances?''

''We run neighboring kingdoms. It's in both of our interests to maintain a cordial relationship.'' The man smiled at her. ''I think that's enough conversation for now.''

''Will you at least tell me where I am?'' Jensen asked.

''I suppose that won't hurt anything. You're in Adjani. But not for long.'' He snapped his fingers and a man standing in the shadows handed her captor the same bottle the nomad had used.

Jensen knew what was coming. "Please, you don't have to do that. I won't give you any trouble."

"You've given us nothing but trouble for all of your waking moments. This simply calms you."

"It knocks me out."

"I won't give you as much."

"Please. I'll stay quiet. You don't have to drug me."

"But you might try to escape."

"I promise not to."

The man smiled. "Nice try, my dear, but I don't believe you."

As he tried to press the bottle against her mouth, Jensen twisted her head back and forth.

His hand slipped away.

He put one hand behind her head and grasped her hair to hold her still and started to clamp the bottle over her face. Jensen's squirming caused him to lose his grip and the liquid spilled all over her face. Jensen saw her chance and brought her teeth down on his hand as hard as she could. He bellowed in pain, then grabbed her throat as he backhanded her across the face.

"Don't you ever do anything to me like that again or so help me I'll kill you. And that's not an empty threat."

He signaled to the other man to hand him the fallen bottle. There was a tiny bit left in the bottom. He got a better grip on Jensen and poured it into her mouth.

Then he sat next to her and watched as her eyes gradually closed.

"You don't understand," he said quietly. "I always get what I want. Always. Did you think you'd be the exception?"

Even in her state, Jensen frowned and raised her hand to her bruised throat.

"You will grow to love me. You'll see. Once we're together, this other man will fade from your memory. There will only be me."

Chapter Twelve

As soon as Michael arrived back at the Adjani house he'd rented, Henry came running out. "Where's Jensen?"

"I don't know," said Michael, his frustration clearly showing. "There's no sign of her."

"What are we going to do?"

"Get in the car."

Ali pulled up behind them just as Henry climbed in. Michael signaled him to follow and in a two-car caravan, they made their way to the outskirts of Adjani at a prearranged meeting spot in the desert.

As they sat in the car waiting for the soldiers, Henry looked at Michael, who clearly was in no mood to talk to anyone. "What do you think has happened to her?"

The muscle in Michael's jaw grew taut with emotion. "I don't know, Henry. I wish to God I did."

"But you have some idea."

"Some idea? I can tell you this. The nomad wasn't interested in Jensen for her cooking skills."

"Too bad," said Henry. "She could have taken out his whole tribe with one of her meat loafs."

Michael just looked at him.

"I'm her brother. I can say that."

"This isn't a joking matter, Henry."

"I know. I'm just afraid if I don't joke, I'll cry. You don't know her, Michael. She's like our mother...such a gentle person. Even if we get her back, she might not be the same."

Michael wasn't even going to consider that. "We'll find her before he has a chance to do anything. She'll be fine."

Henry looked sideways at his friend. "You're taking this very personally, considering you barely know Jensen. What's going on with you?"

Michael stared straight ahead through the windshield of his stopped car. "Why do you ask?"

"Because you've always been the calmest man I know, and right now you seem to be doing all you can not to explode."

The muscle in his jaw moved again. "Jensen and I have had a chance to get to know each other quite well over the past few days. We've spent a lot of time together."

"And?"

"I'm in love with her."

"But you've only known her a few days."

Michael turned toward Henry. "She's your sister. You know her better than anyone else. How long do you think it should take a man to fall in love with her?"

A smile curled a corner of Henry's mouth. "You're absolutely right. She's adorable."

"And we're going to get her back." Michael leaned forward in his seat and peered into the distance. "There they are."

Ali, Henry and Michael climbed out of their cars and walked toward the long caravan of cars and trucks. As soon as they parked, more than a dozen men poured out, all of them soldiers, but in plainclothes.

Young Yusef was with them.

He ran ahead to Michael. "I heard men talk in taxi! I know who has lady."

"What men?" asked Michael.

"Men who work for Sheik Ahmed of Adjani."

"What did you hear?"

"They were laughing, saying how they had fooled the lady, that she is stupid, like all Americans, that Sheik Ahmed had tricked her into coming to Sumaru just as they had tricked her into going into the desert. They talked about how she had made them rich men."

"Who were these men?" Henry asked.

"Yusef doesn't know. Never saw them before. But they work for Sheik Ahmed. They said so. I heard them."

"Have you told anyone else?" asked Michael.

"No, sir. Only you."

"Keep it that way."

"Yes, sir."

"What do we do now?" Henry asked.

"Move very carefully," said Michael. "The guy is powerful and, some would say, one brick short of a load."

"Would he hurt Jensen?"

"In a heartbeat."

"We have to go after him."

"But it can't be obvious. We don't want to do anything to arouse his suspicions."

"Just tell me what to do," said Henry. "I'm there."

Michael shook his head. "I think it's best if you do nothing. If Yusef is right, you were set up by Ahmed to lure Jensen here. That means he knows who you are. The last thing we want is for you to be anywhere near him."

"But he has to be confronted."

"That's right. By me. Not you."

"I'm her brother," said Henry.

"It has to be done diplomatically, and by someone of his own station. You've been around here enough to understand that, Henry. I'm going to send you and Yusef to my home with one of my men." He signaled to a young man nearby and spoke to him in Arabic.

"What will you say?" asked Henry.

"I don't want Ahmed to know that I suspect him of having Jensen. I want to try to draw him in on the search. The less he thinks he's suspected, the more open he's likely to be."

"I should be there," Henry said.

Michael put his hands on Henry's shoulders. "I know you want to be, but it's not wise. You're considered an escaped prisoner. If you're recognized and arrested again, we'll lose time in our search for Jensen—time we can ill afford at this point. And you can bet they won't let you get away as easily the second time."

"But..."

"I'm going to find her, Henry. You can count on it. You can count on me."

Henry looked at his friend for a long moment. If there was one thing he knew about Michael Hassan, it was that he was a man of his word. He always had been, even in college. The rest of the group they ran with were a bunch of irresponsible drunks. But Michael was a rock. He always did what he said, and he took care of his own. Henry couldn't even remember how many scrapes Michael had saved him from.

He trusted Michael with his life.

He trusted him with Jensen's life.

"All right," Henry said. "Just find her quickly before something happens to her."

As Henry was led off, Michael turned to the rest of the men. "I want all of you to go into the city of Adjani, some in pairs, some of you alone, spread out and start asking questions. Did the minister give you Miss O'Hara's description?"

The men all nodded.

"Time is critical. I don't even know if she's still there. Start on the outskirts of the city and work your way toward the center of the town.'' He looked at Yusef who was still standing there. ''I thought I told you to go with Henry.''

''No,'' he said, his skinny arms folded across his chest. Then he looked down. ''No, sir.''

''You've done well, Yusef, but there's nothing more you can do. Go with Miss O'Hara's brother.''

''I'm sorry to disobey, but I'm going with you. If you won't let me, then I go to Adjani alone. She's nice lady. I find her.''

Michael knew the kid was serious and he didn't have time to argue with him. ''All right. But you have to stay with me. I don't want you taking off on your own.''

''Yes, sir.''

''And I want you out of Western dress.'' He looked at Ali. ''Do you have anything he can wear?''

Ali cleared his throat. ''Miss O'Hara's clothing— the robe and headdress. They're in the car.''

Michael flinched inwardly, but no one looking at him would have known.

''Yusef, you go with Ali and put on the clothes. Once we arrive at Ahmed's palace, stay out of sight until we're inside the gates. Once Ali and I are inside the palace itself, you get out of the car and look around as much as you can around the outside of the building. If Jensen is there, she's inside. Check windows. Do you have a watch?''

He proudly held up his wrist.

''Good. From the time we enter the palace, you take exactly half an hour to look around, then return to the car. Don't be any longer than that. Understand?''

"Yes, sir."

"Any questions?"

"What if someone sees me?"

"Behave as if you belong there. Don't show fear or awkwardness under any circumstances."

"Yes, sir."

"Ali, once we're inside, I want you to look around as much as possible. I'll be with Ahmed. You make some excuse to be somewhere else. There will be guards, so your access will be limited and your appearance is much more conspicuous than Yusef's. Just do what you can."

He inclined his head.

"Let's go."

As Ali and Yusef climbed into one of the cars, Ali reached into the back seat for Jensen's robe and headdress, and handed them to the boy. "Put these on."

"Yes, sir."

"And don't talk to me."

"Yes, sir."

Michael took the lead with Ali right behind him.

They went straight back into the city and traveled within its walls to the outskirts where an elaborate palace sat regally on the edge of the desert. Michael was stopped at the gate by two armed guards.

As soon as they looked in the car window, they knew who he was and executed sharp bows.

"I need to see King Ahmed."

One of the solders inclined his head toward the second car. ''Who is he?''

''My bodyguard.''

''Of course. I'll tell the king you're here. He'll wish to know what your business with him is.''

''I want to enlist his help in finding a young woman who recently disappeared from Adjani.''

Michael knew Ahmed well enough to understand that he'd find that kind of request too amusing to turn away, particularly if Yusef was right.

''And please apologize to him for the informality of my visit, but there's no time to waste.''

''Yes, sir.''

Both soldiers, backs straight, marched away. While one stood at the gate, his gun at his side, the other went into a small booth and made a phone call.

Michael literally held his breath. Jensen was there. He knew it. He could feel it; feel her presence.

The soldier in the booth signaled the other. That one waved Michael and Ali through the gate.

Once inside, Michael, who had been there many times before, took the drive around to the other side of the palace and parked. A guard greeted them at the door.

''Your Highness,'' he said with a bow. ''I'm to show you into the living area. Sheik Ahmed will be with you soon.''

Ali and Michael followed the guard into a very Western-looking room.

''Excuse me,'' said Michael before the guard could leave, ''but would you please show my body-guard where the bathroom is.''

"Of course. Follow me, please."

Ali inclined his head toward Michael and followed the guard out.

That left Michael to pace helplessly while he waited for Ahmed.

Ahmed walked into Jensen's room and sat on the edge of the bed staring down at her unconscious figure. "Well, well, it appears you've made friends in high places. I thought Michael's rescue of you in the desert was a fluke, but apparently not.

Jensen's eyes fluttered open. "What?"

"You seem to have bewitched the king of my neighboring country just as you bewitched me. Could Michael be the man you spoke of earlier?"

"I don't know what you're talking about."

"He is here, apparently, in an effort to enlist me in the search for you. How ironic is that, my dear?"

She tried to sit up. "Michael is here?"

Ahmed put his hand on her shoulder and shoved her back on the bed. "That's right. But he'll be leaving soon enough, assured of my concern and a generous offer of assistance."

Jensen looked at him blurrily through heavy-lidded eyes. "What do you hope is going to happen? Do you think I'm going to suddenly fall in love with you?"

"Love isn't a requirement for what I have in mind. But I feel confident you'll come around."

"You're a pathetic man, Ahmed. I'll never feel anything but contempt for you."

His eyes narrowed. "You had better watch what

you say and remember the power of the man to whom you are saying it.''

"What more could you possibly do to me? You've already stripped me of my freedom."

"You'll find out soon enough."

She watched as he rose from the bed and went to a chest where a horribly familiar bottle of liquid rested.

"We had to get a new one, since you spilled most of the other," he explained.

Jensen was feeling remarkably calm. Perhaps it was because Michael was nearby.

Perhaps she'd simply found her courage.

She just knew that something inside her had changed.

"Tell me, Ahmed, have you ever had a woman you didn't have to kidnap and drug? I mean, one who liked you well enough to come with you of her own volition?"

He didn't answer, but Jensen could see the anger etched in the lines of his profile and she reveled in it.

"I imagine the people who know what you've done—and there must be many—are laughing behind your back."

"They wouldn't dare," he said angrily as he picked up the bottle and removed the cap.

Jensen had a plan. She was going to appear to drink the vile potion, then spit it out as soon as Ahmed left.

So this time, when Ahmed grabbed her hair to jerk her head back, Jensen gave him a token struggle so she wouldn't arouse suspicion. He forced the bottle into her mouth and poured.

Jensen gave the appearance of swallowing. In fact, a little did trickle down her throat. But she held most of it in her mouth.

But Ahmed didn't leave. He just sat there, staring at her.

"How stupid do you think I am?" he asked.

Jensen didn't say anything. She couldn't. Her mouth was full.

Ahmed pinched her nose to cut off her air. Now Jensen really struggled, but with her hands and feet bound, there was really nothing she could do.

She swallowed for real.

Ahmed smiled victoriously.

Jensen fought to stay alert. Michael was here. If she couldn't call to him, he'd never know. He'd leave without her.

But she could feel herself losing control of her body as her limbs grew weak and blackness enveloped her.

As soon as her body went limp, Ahmed screwed the lid back on the bottle and set it down. He sat staring at her, his gaze moving over each lovely feature of her face. What he was doing was completely irrational. He knew it. He'd never done anything like this in his life.

But he'd known the moment he saw Jensen that he had to have her. And this was the only way.

He reached out and touched her cheek. "Whether you want to believe it or not," he said softly, "you will be mine, in body and soul. You will grow to love me.''

Rising from the bed, he took a last look back at her and left to meet with Michael.

Unbidden, unnoticed, tears rolled down her pale cheeks.

''Hello, Michael,'' Ahmed said cheerfully when he walked into the room. ''It's been a long time. I'm sorry about keeping you waiting so long. So what exactly is it that you want to see me about?''

Michael watched his reactions carefully. ''A missing American woman. Her name is Jensen O'Hara. She's the sister of a friend of mine and she was abducted off the streets of Adjani. I need help to find her. I need your help.''

''Of course, of course,'' he said in a friendly fashion. ''Tell me what I can do.'' He waved Michael into a chair.

Michael inclined his head toward Ahmed's hand. There was a perfect set of teeth marks. ''That looks painful.''

Ahmed looked at it and shrugged. ''It's nothing. A little accident. Now tell me exactly what you want.''

''I'd like you to have your men blanket the city to interview people about whether or not they've seen her.''

''Blanket the city. That's a lot of manpower. What's this woman to you?''

''I told you. She's my friend's sister.''

''And that's all?''

"That's enough. So will you help?"

"Absolutely. I myself am leaving the city for my other palace in less than an hour. But I'll make sure men are dispatched immediately and I'll have you updated as they report in."

"Thank you."

"If there's anything else, don't hesitate to ask. It's important that we maintain the high level of cooperation between our countries that existed in your father's time."

"I agree."

"Good." He rose, indicating that Michael should rise also. "You'll pardon me if I don't walk you to the door. I have some arrangements to make."

"Of course."

Ali was waiting at attention outside the door when Michael stepped out. Wordlessly the two of them walked through the foyer and outside into the stifling heat.

"Well?" asked Michael under his breath as they walked.

"I saw nothing," said Ali, "but I wasn't allowed to move freely. The guard kept an eye on me."

"She's here," said Michael. "I know it with every fiber of my being. She's in that palace."

"How can you be sure?"

"I can feel it. But more importantly, there's physical evidence that Ahmed has had contact with her."

"What evidence?"

Michael held up his hand where Jensen's teeth marks had faded, but were still visible. "Ahmed and I have matching scars. Jensen has a way of leaving her mark on men who touch her without her permission.''

"What do we do now?'' asked Ali. "If, as you believe, she's in there, we can't leave without her.''

"Go to your car. We'll discuss the matter later when we meet outside the gates.''

Ali was clearly reluctant, but did as he was told.

"Your Highness,'' said Yusef from the floor of the back seat of Michael's car as soon as the door was closed.

"Did you see anything?''

"No, sir. And I went all the way around the palace.''

"I didn't expect you would, but thank you for trying. Now I need you to do another service for me.''

"Of course.''

"Drive this car out of here for me.''

"What about you?''

"I'm going to be flying out.''

"How?''

"There's no time to explain now. I want you to meet with Ali outside the gates—well outside the gates—and then I want both of you to return to my desert home. I'll see you there. In fact, I'll probably get there before you.''

"What about lady?''

"She'll be with me.''

Yusef didn't ask how that was possible. If his king said it was so, then it was so.

"Shouldn't Ali stay with you?''

"No. The guards need to see two cars leaving. There will be no way for Ali to return unnoticed."

"Perhaps Ali should stay and you should leave."

"I'm a pilot, and that's what is needed for this. Ali is not."

Yusef nodded. "Still, I'm surprised he would leave you."

"He doesn't know it yet. And I'd appreciate your discretion in the matter for as long as possible."

"Yes, sir."

Michael looked around to see if anyone was watching. "Ready?"

"Yes."

"You're a fine young man, Yusef."

Yusef beamed.

Michael climbed out of the car and Yusef instantly took his place behind the wheel. Ali, who had already turned his car around and started down the driveway, saw nothing.

Michael took a cushion from the back seat and put it under Yusef. "Much better," he said. "Now be careful."

"Yes, sir. Yusef is always careful." The next moment, the car was in gear and following Ali.

Michael stepped away from the car and stared at the palace as he slipped on a pair of sunglasses to hide his blue eyes. He knew this palace well. He'd flown here many times over the years with his father and brother.

He'd played here as a child.

Jensen was in there.

His Jensen.

And he was going to get her out safely so she could come home to him.

A corner of his mouth lifted ironically.

Come home to him. That was impossible, of course. Jensen wasn't his. She never could be.

Michael headed for the tarmac.

He had to admit it was impressive. Ahmed had done a good job of building an airport in the middle of nowhere. It must have cost him a fortune.

Ahmed and his family had always spent lavishly on themselves. Their palace had every accommodation one could think of. Their cars were only the best and their private fleet of jets and yachts would have made the richest of men proud.

Michael's father had a tradition of giving back to his people through schools and special programs. That was the way Michael intended to handle things.

As he approached the large private jet waiting on the runway, he inclined his head toward the workers. In the robes, he looked like anyone and everyone.

The stairway into the jet was down.

Michael climbed aboard as though he belonged there and did a walk-through on the jet.

No one was there.

Then he went to the cockpit. The pilot was there, getting things ready for takeoff.

"What time are we leaving?" asked Michael.

"Who are you?"

"One of the passengers."

The pilot nodded. "Probably in another fifteen minutes. Thirty at most."

Michael stepped further into the cockpit.

The pilot looked up. "Is there something else?"

"Nothing important." And with that, Michael reached out and grasped a pressure point on the man's neck, rendering him almost instantly unconscious. Serving in his country's air force had its advantages. He'd have to teach that one to Jensen.

Chapter Thirteen

A hand came down on Michael's shoulder. He turned, ready to do battle, only to find Ali standing there in a white robe. "What are you doing here?"

"My job." He inclined his head toward the unconscious pilot. "What now?"

"We hide him."

"I'll take care of that," said Ali as he leaned over the pilot, picked him up and threw him over his shoulders as if he were a sack of flour.

"Make sure he's bound and gagged," said Michael. "He'll be coming to in a little while."

Michael slid into the pilot's seat and began doing an instrumentation check.

As he sat there, the copilot arrived. Before anything could be said, Ali was behind him. He met the same fate as the pilot and was carried away by Ali.

As Ali returned to the cockpit and sat beside Michael, he touched Michael's arm and inclined his head toward the tarmac. A long, black Mercedes was making its way toward the jet.

Michael stared intently at the car as it stopped near the stairs. Where was Jensen?

Sheik Ahmed and three other men got out, two of them presumably bodyguards. While three of the men boarded the jet, the driver reached into the back seat of the car and lifted an obviously unconscious, robed and heavily veiled woman into his arms.

Michael, his body rigid, started to rise, his anger a palpable presence in the cockpit.

Ali put his hand on Michael's arm to hold him in place. "We must get her to safety first. Then we'll take care of other business."

Michael retook his seat.

Ahmed's voice came on over the intercom. "Let's go."

Michael inclined his head toward Ali, who left the cockpit and secured the outer door, ignored by the others on the jet, then returned to sit beside Michael.

"Where are we supposed to be going?" asked Ali.

Michael pointed at a map. "Cairo."

"And instead, we're going?"

"My desert palace." The jet engines whined as Michael moved into position for takeoff.

"So what you're saying," said Ali, "is that we have a jet full of hostages?"

"Not full."

"How do you propose to keep them at bay when they realize where we're headed?"

"That's where you come in," said Michael.

Ali lifted a dark brow. "You don't ask much."

"The key is going to be to make sure Jensen is protected. At my signal, you go back into the jet on a walk-through and position yourself near her so she can't be used as a shield."

"They'll have the guns. I have only a dagger."

"That's a problem," admitted Michael.

"And I would guess that you have no weapon at all."

"Just my hands."

Ali strapped himself into the copilot's seat. "The flight will be short, but it's going to be a long landing."

"Get ready," said Michael as the jet began its race down the runway and rose smoothly into the air.

Michael waited a little longer than he normally would have to bank the jet to the left, and then tried to do it in such a gentle fashion that a passenger wouldn't notice it unless they were paying close attention.

It was only thirty minutes to the runway at his palace at Sumaru. He used the radio to get through to his minister of defense.

"Where are you, Your Highness?"

"I'm afraid you're not going to like the answer."

"Like it or not, I need to know. We've had no luck in locating the elusive Miss O'Hara."

"She's with me. You can call the men back from Adjani."

"Yes, sir."

"I need you to assemble enough armed men on the runway at my desert palace to make a show of force, and I need them there in about twenty-five minutes."

"What on earth for?"

"It seems I've hijacked the sheik of Adjani's jet, along with the sheik and his party."

The minister collapsed into the chair that was luckily behind him. "You have done what?"

"I think you heard me correctly the first time. There's no time to repeat."

"But, Your Highness, surely you know that this is an act of war. We could be attacked for this."

"We could be," Michael agreed, "but I don't think we will. If what he's done with Miss O'Hara becomes known publicly, Sheik Ahmed will suffer public ridicule and humiliation. On the other hand, if he lets this incident pass quietly, he can avoid becoming a laughingstock. So get those men out there. We'll be landing soon."

"Yes, sir."

Michael disconnected and he and Ali spent the next twenty minutes flying in silence.

Then Michael looked at Ali and inclined his head. "It's time."

Wordlessly Ali left his seat and headed into the cabin of the jet. To Ahmed and his men, Ali was no one. Just another employee. No one bothered to look up.

Jensen was alone in the last aisle of the jet, lying unconscious on a couch, her hands and ankles bound. The veil had been lifted and he could see the bruises on her face and throat.

Ali could do nothing at the moment but look at her, but Jensen, had she known, would have been touched by the gentleness in his eyes.

As the jet began to descend, the four men looked out the window. Sheik Ahmed flicked an irritated finger at one of the men. "Find out what's going on."

Ali rethought his position. Jensen would be safe enough if the men could be kept under control.

There was the rub.

He moved forward to stand behind Ahmed, whipped the headdress off the sheik's head, grabbed his hair to stretch his neck and put his dagger at the man's throat. "Don't move," he said calmly.

The man who'd been about to go to the cockpit sat back down, his eyes wide.

"What do you want?" asked Ahmed, panic sounding in his voice. "If it's money, I have plenty. Just name the amount."

"Shut up," said Ali. "If everyone does exactly as I say, no one will get hurt. You," he said to the man farthest from him. "Remove your weapon with your left thumb and forefinger and toss it into the aisle."

The man did.

"Now the rest of you, one at a time. And if any one of you tries anything, you may well get me, but not before I get your sheik. Understand?"

"Do what he says," ordered the sheik.

Each of the men put his gun in the aisle.

"Now sit down and fasten your seat belts. We're going to be landing in a few minutes." He looked down at the sheik. "My dagger is a sharp one. You had better hope it's a smooth landing."

Ali kept his grip on Ahmed as Michael set the jet down in one smooth motion, as Ali had known he would.

As soon as Ahmed saw the palace in the distance, he swore under his breath. "Michael Hassan."

"That's right," said Ali.

"But why?"

"It appears you took something that didn't belong to you."

"The woman? He's doing this for a woman?"

Ali raised a dark brow. "You are one to talk."

As the jet rolled to a stop, it was suddenly surrounded by armed soldiers.

"I can't believe this," said Ahmed. "This is tantamount to a declaration of war."

Michael heard him as he walked out of the cockpit. "It's whatever you want it to be," said Michael. "One way or another, I'm taking Jensen with me. You can humiliate yourself by making public the fact that the only way you can get a woman is to kidnap her, which declaring war would do, or you can let it go right here and now."

Ahmed still had the dagger to his throat. At a signal from Michael, Ali lowered the dagger to his side, but kept his eyes on the other men, still strapped into their seats.

"What's it going to be?" asked Michael.

Ali gathered up the guns and tied them into the cloth from Ahmed's headdress.

Ahmed was clearly furious, but there was nothing he could do. "Take her. That will be the end of it."

"One more thing," said Michael.

Ahmed waited, his eyes blazing.

"I want Adjani's slave trade dismantled."

"It can't be done," snarled Ahmed. "It's a tradition that goes back more than a thousand years."

"You can and you will. Or, if you find it problematic, I can have my armed forces give you a hand."

"Another threat?"

"I don't threaten. But I'll tell you that there are things in our world that are going to change under my watch."

"Then let's all pray you have a very short watch."

"You'd better pray it's a long one," said Ali, "because if anything happens to my king, you're the first person I'll come looking for. Is that understood?"

Ahmed took several deep breaths. "Understood."

Michael started to walk past him to the back of the jet, but Ali stopped him. "You take these," he said, handing him the guns. "I'll get Miss O'Hara."

"Don't be ridiculous," said Michael as he started past him. "I'll get her."

Ali caught his arm in a firm grip. "She was taken because I made mistakes. I'd like to be the one to carry her off the plane, if you don't mind."

There was something in Ali's tone that Michael chose not to argue with. "All right."

"Thank you."

"Your pilot and copilot are tied up in rear storage," said Michael as he walked toward the front of the jet. "They should be able to fly you home now. I wouldn't linger here if I were you."

As soon as he stepped off the jet, Michael walked to the highest ranking officer there and handed him the guns. "Get rid of these. Keep the men here until the jet takes off."

"Yes, sir."

Then Michael turned and waited while Ali came down the stairs carrying a still unconscious Jensen in his arms, her veil replaced to cover her face.

Ali handed her into Michael's waiting arms. "You get her home. I'll finish up here." Then he handed Michael his dagger. "You'll need this to free her."

Michael climbed into the rear of the waiting car with Jensen. As it started toward the palace, the first thing he did was cut the ropes from her wrists and ankles. Then he pushed the veils away from her face.

The moment he saw her beautiful, bruised face he yelled at the driver to stop the car. He had opened the door, fully intending to run back to the jet and pound Ahmed into the tarmac when Jensen's eyes opened.

"Michael?" she said, her voice small and raspy.

He stopped.

Tears spilled from the corners of her eyes. "I didn't think I'd ever see you again," she whispered.

He pushed her hair away from her face. "I'm here. But there's something I have to do...."

Jensen grasped his hand. "Don't leave me."

His gaze moved over her face. "Ahmed hurt you. I can't let him get away with that."

"Please," she whispered. "I'm afraid."

He cradled her in his arms. "Don't be. I'm right here and I'm not going anywhere."

Her eyes started to drift closed, but she opened them again. "Is Henry all right?"

"He's fine. He's on his way here now. He should arrive in just a few hours."

"Thank you." Jensen tried to smile, but it hurt her face and she winced.

"Just be still. We'll get you fixed up."

Her gaze locked with his. "I knew you'd find me."

A corner of his mouth lifted. "Then you knew more than I did. Now close your eyes and rest."

Jensen did as she was told and sighed deeply, safe in the arms of her man. "I love you," she said softly.

Michael gazed at her as the car moved toward the palace. "I love you, too," he said when he thought she couldn't hear. "More than I ever thought it was possible to love anyone."

When the driver stopped the car, Michael carried Jensen inside and straight to his quarters. He didn't care what anyone said; what anyone thought. He wasn't going to let her out of his sight.

A manservant followed him. "Get a doctor here right now," Michael said.

The man bowed and left.

Michael lay Jensen on his bed and began undressing her.

The more he saw, the angrier he got. She had apparently put up quite a fight. Her arms were bruised; her back; her shoulders. He touched his fingertips to the ugly purplish marks on her throat where she'd clearly been choked.

Her wrists were raw where she'd tried to escape her bonds. Even her ankles had marks.

"Oh, Jensen," he whispered, "I'm so sorry I didn't protect you the way I should have."

He'd never felt such anger. If Ahmed had been in the room with him...

But he wasn't.

Michael locked the door to keep people from walking in, then poured some water into a basin and gently sponged her body clean.

When he'd finished, he pulled a sheet up to her bare shoulders and sat on the bed beside her, her hand in his, stroking her fingers.

There was a knock on the door.

"Who is it?"

"Ali."

"It's locked. Use your key."

"How is she?" asked Ali as he walked into the room.

"Battered." He looked at Ali. "You knew, didn't you? That's why you didn't want me to carry her off the plane."

"I saw her face. I knew what you'd do if you saw it."

Michael nodded.

"This is my fault," said Ali. "You asked me to take care of her and I failed."

"You couldn't have known what Ahmed was up to."

"But I should have been more alert when she stopped the car to pick me up."

Jensen opened her eyes again. The drug just wouldn't let her out of its grip. But she saw Ali and she smiled at him. "Oh, I'm so glad to see you're all right. I was worried about you."

Ali moved forward and returned the smile. "I'm fine. Now we must get you better."

"I meant to tell you earlier how perfectly beautiful your English is." She held up her free hand and he took it in his. Emotion was clearly visible in his usually stern face.

"How are you feeling?"

"Tired. I can't stay awake."

"Then perhaps you should sleep."

"I don't seem to have much choice." Her gaze moved to Michael and stayed there as her eyelids drifted closed.

Ali put his hand on Michael's shoulder and squeezed. "Is there anything I can do?"

"Get some rest, Ali. It's been a long few days."

"Yes, sir. What about you?"

"I'm not leaving Jensen."

Ali nodded. "I'll be nearby if you need me."

Michael stopped him just before the door closed. "Ali, where is Yusef?"

"I placed him with a soldier before returning to Ahmed's palace. He's fine. I sent him back to the city."

"I told him he'd be coming here."

"I thought it was best to return him to his uncle until things were settled."

Michael nodded. "Two things. I want a new taxi given to his uncle. And Yusef is to be given whatever he wants."

"I'll see that it's done."

"Thank you."

"Do you want the door locked again?"

"No."

Michael sat alone, his eyes never leaving Jensen. He ran the tip of his finger over her exposed collarbone and the soft skin of her shoulder.

He didn't turn when the door opened. He assumed it was Ali until he heard the swish of silken robes. When he looked up, it was to find Ayalah across the bed from him.

"You shouldn't be here," said Michael.

"No one saw me. How is she?"

"The doctor hasn't been here yet. She's bruised and she's obviously been drugged. I think she'll be all right, though."

"You love her very much, don't you?" said Ayalah softly.

"Yes," he said simply.

"You should be with her."

Michael looked up at the woman who was to be his wife. "You know that's impossible."

"It's not right that you should be without the woman you love and I should be without the man I love."

"You love someone else?"

She didn't meet Michael's gaze, but looked down at Jensen and nodded. "He is no one important. The son of a diplomat. We met by accident and fell in love. Neither of us meant for it to happen—but then one seldom loves where it is intended."

"I'm sorry," said Michael.

"It is a tragedy for both of us."

"We shouldn't be speaking of this, Ayalah. We shouldn't be speaking at all. It goes against everything that's expected of us."

It was as though she hadn't heard him. "What are we going to do?"

"You know what will happen if we don't marry. We will dishonor both of our families. You will be disowned and unwelcome in your father's house."

"But if I make my own home with the man I love, will that matter so much?"

"Can you live with never seeing any of your family again? You will be dead to them."

"It is a dark thought that I've struggled with for many months."

"Can you live with their dishonor?"

She peered at Michael over the top of her veil. "I think that is more your dilemma than mine. You would dishonor the memory of your family. They can't argue with you or fight back. Their honor is your honor. You must do what they expected of you."

Michael sighed. "You should go back to your quarters before you're missed, Ayalah."

She nodded. "I just want you to understand that I know how you feel. And I wanted to wish your woman well."

Michael didn't watch as she left the room, but kept his eyes on Jensen, pushing the hair from her face. The stain had worn off. Either that, or her own color had grown so pale even the stain couldn't hide it any longer.

Michael lay on the bed beside Jensen and pulled her into his arms. He needed to hold her so badly it hurt.

"Michael?" said Jensen.

He rubbed his lips against her hair. "Mmm?"

"What are you doing?"

"Holding you."

She snuggled against him. "That's nice. I wish we could stay like this."

"I know."

Jensen's breathing grew deep and even. Michael knew she'd fallen asleep again. She had a knack of doing that whenever she was in his arms.

He kissed her forehead and held her closer.

When the doctor entered, Michael was still there, and didn't rise immediately despite the man's disapproving look.

"What happened to her?" asked the doctor as he moved further into the room.

"She's been beaten and drugged."

"What drug?"

"I don't know."

"I'll draw blood and have it analyzed, but my guess is that it will wear away quite harmlessly on its own. Get off the bed, please, so I can examine her."

Michael reluctantly slid off, but he held on to her hand while the doctor pulled back the sheet limb by limb and went over every bruise on her body.

Michael truly hated having another man touch her. Even a doctor.

"She's fine," he said when he'd finished his inspection. "I imagine she'll be quite sore for a few days, but nothing is broken."

He put salve and bandages on her raw wrists. "These will take a little longer, and might leave scars. Make sure they're kept clean."

"I will." Michael cleared his throat. He hated to ask the next question, but it had to be done. "Can you tell if she was raped?"

"Not without an internal examination. Do you have reason to believe she was?"

"I don't know one way or the other. Jensen hasn't said anything about it, but I think she's been unconscious for most of her imprisonment. I don't think she would even know."

"Do you want me to check her?"

"It's not up to me." He leaned over Jensen and shook her shoulder. "Darling, wake up."

Nothing.

"Come on, Jensen. Just for a minute."

Her eyes fluttered open.

"There's a doctor here. He's been giving you an examination."

She focused on the strange man in the room. "How am I?"

"Fine, as far as I can tell."

She looked back at Michael. "Is there a problem?"

He touched her face as he leaned closer to her. "Do you know if you were—mistreated—in any other way?"

"Are you asking if I was raped?"

"Yes."

"I don't think so. Not that I'm aware of."

"Do you want the doctor to check you?"

She looked into Michael's eyes. "I guess he should."

"Do you want me here?"

She nodded and held up her hand while the doctor positioned the sheet and had her raise her knees.

Michael stared straight back into her eyes as he tightly held her hand.

"What if I was?" she asked. "How will you feel about me then?"

"I love you," he whispered. "Nothing is going to change that."

She closed her eyes.

"Are you almost finished," he asked the doctor harshly.

The doctor straightened her knees and pulled the sheet down. "There's no tearing or bruising. I'd say that, while she was handled roughly, she wasn't raped."

"Thank you, Doctor," said Michael. "You can leave now. If you find she needs anything after you've analyzed the blood you've drawn, I expect you to come immediately."

"Of course, Your Highness."

"And I expect your complete discretion."

"You may be assured of it."

When he'd gone, Michael lay his head beside hers on the pillow. "Oh, Jensen, you break my heart every time I look at you, every time I think of you. How can I let you go?"

Chapter Fourteen

Henry came flying into the bedroom. "Jensen?"

Michael was back in the chair beside the bed. He rose quickly and put his finger to his lips. "She's sleeping."

"Is she all right?" whispered Henry as he moved closer.

"She will be."

He looked down at the sleeping face of his cherished sister. "Oh, my God," he said when he saw the bruises. "How long has she been unconscious?"

"She's in and out."

"Has a doctor seen her?"

"Yes. She's going to be fine."

Henry touched Jensen's hair. "Was she...was she..." He left the word unspoken.

"No," said Michael. "If she had been, Ahmed would be a dead man now."

Henry nodded. "I didn't want to admit how worried about her I was until I knew she was safe. She might be my baby sister, but she's always been my rock. My anchor."

Michael said nothing.

"I don't know what I would have done if you hadn't been able to find her. Thank you, Michael. I'll sit with her now."

"It's all right, Henry. I don't mind being here at all. You must need to rest after your journey."

Henry slapped his friend's shoulder. "Get out of here and let me sit with my sister. You have a country to run."

Michael reluctantly rose from the chair, his eyes on Jensen. "Let me know if anything changes."

"Of course."

"I'll come back in a little while so you can take a break."

Michael went to another section of his quarters, showered and changed into jeans and a long-sleeved white shirt, then went to his office where a mountain of mail, faxes and telephone messages waited for him.

His male secretary followed him, speaking a mile a minute in Arabic. Michael answered with short sentences, sat behind his desk and got to work.

And work he did, for hours, doing his best to shut out the fact that Jensen was down the hall.

Doing his best to shut out the knowledge that he

was going to have to send her away and never see her again.

He did everything but return the phone calls. Those could be deferred to another day.

Then he sent his secretary away.

What Michael wanted—what he needed—was time alone; time to think.

"Michael?" said Nira from the doorway.

He looked at his sister and inwardly sighed. "What is it?"

"I think we need to talk."

"About what?"

"May I come in? Your secretary is about to have a stroke because I'm in this part of the house."

"Of course."

She closed the door behind her.

"I want to offer you my congratulations on finding Henry and bringing his sister back safely."

"Thank you."

"You know, of course, that you must now send her away."

Michael held on to his temper as he rose from his chair. "I don't want to discuss this with you, Nira."

"I'm your family. The only family you have left. Who else will you discuss this inappropriate attachment with?"

"Nira, this is none of your business."

"It is my business if you disgrace our family name. The repercussions don't just affect you, my brother. They affect me and my chances for a successful marriage."

"Not if the man you choose to spend your life

with is worthwhile and has enough character to marry you the woman and not the Hassan family.''

"You know that has nothing to do with it. Things here are the way they've been for centuries. It isn't for you or me to suddenly change them. Not even our mother could do that.''

"Our mother was American.''

"And our father didn't have a woman he was already engaged to when he met our mother. He wasn't king. He was free in a way you'll never be again.''

"You think I don't know this?'' he asked evenly. "You think this hasn't haunted my every waking thought since I met Jensen?''

"Then I have your word that you won't be doing anything foolish? I can count on this?''

"Nira,'' Michael said in measured tones, "you're my sister and I respect your feelings and wishes, but my relationship with Jensen O'Hara—or any other woman—is none of your business and I will not discuss it with you. Go back to your own quarters.''

She shook her head. "You're going to throw everything away for her, aren't you?''

Michael said nothing.

"You can't do this to your people. They'll be swallowed up by the likes of Ahmed. There's no one to step into your shoes.''

"I know what my responsibilities are. And I know what the consequences of my actions—whatever they are—will be.''

"Michael, I beg you...''

"Go, Nira.''

His sister stared at him for several seconds before turning and leaving the room.

Michael just sat there, his heart so heavy in his chest that he felt bowed by the weight.

Rising from his chair with a sigh, he went to his bedroom where Jensen still lay with Henry at her side. He had fallen asleep, his head on the mattress.

Michael touched his shoulder. "Henry?"

Henry raised his head, his eyes bleary with sleep.

"Go to bed. I'll stay with her for the rest of the night."

Henry looked at his sister and touched her hand, then rose from the chair. "I'll come back in a few hours."

"Don't worry about it. I want to stay with her."

Henry nodded. "I understand. Take good care of her."

"I will."

As soon as Henry had gone, Michael turned off all the lights except one on a table across the room, then sat on the edge of the bed and just watched Jensen sleep.

He wanted to memorize every feature; every expression; the sound of her breathing; the way her dark eyelashes fanned her flushed cheeks and contrasted with her blond hair; the contour of her jaw; the fullness of her lips and that hint of a dimple at the corner of her mouth that was evident even in sleep.

Never had he known anything with the absolute certainty that he knew he loved this woman with everything in him.

How on earth was he going to get through the rest of his life without her?

Jensen opened her eyes and looked directly into his. A gentle smile curved her mouth. "Hello," she said softly.

Michael brushed his hand gently over her forehead to push her hair back. "Hello."

"What are you doing?"

"Watching you sleep."

"It must be a slow night at the palace."

A corner of his mouth lifted. "How are you feeling?"

"Better."

"Good. The drugs must be wearing off."

Michael started to rise from the bed, but Jensen caught his hand. "Are you leaving?"

"No. I was just going to move to the chair."

"Please lie with me."

"It's not such a good idea, Jensen. Someone might walk in."

"I'm not asking that you make love to me. Just hold me. Unless you don't want to."

Michael touched the curve of her hip. "Move over."

Jensen did, but it caused her to wince.

"Are you all right?"

"Just sore."

He lay beside her, his arm behind her head, and pulled her back against his chest. "Try to sleep," he said. "Give yourself as much time to heal as possible."

Jensen sighed. "I love being in your arms."

Michael rubbed his cheek against her hair but didn't say anything.

"You're going to send me away, aren't you?"

"Yes."

"What if I refuse to leave?"

"I'll have you escorted."

"You love me, Michael. You know you do."

He said nothing.

She turned her head and looked at him. "Don't you?"

"This isn't the right time to discuss this."

"I understand you have obligations."

"No, Jensen, you don't. You come from a completely different culture. You have no idea what my obligations are or what effect my failing to meet them will have on thousands of people."

"Michael…"

He put his lips against her ear. "Go to sleep."

"Promise me you won't leave me."

"I'll stay with you tonight."

That had to be enough for the moment.

"Hold me closer," she said.

Michael pulled her body closer to his, his arm around her waist, her back against his chest.

Jensen just had a feeling. She couldn't explain it. "I'm not going to see you again after tonight, am I?"

There was a long hesitation. "No. You'll be staying here until you're healed. I'll be returning to the city palace in the morning."

"Why?"

"I have business…."

Jensen turned to face him, wincing with every movement. "Don't lie to me, Michael. You're leaving to get away from me."

Their faces were inches apart. "All right. No lies. That's exactly why I'm leaving."

"You love me."

"Yes."

"I understand that we can't be together in a traditional sense, that I'll never be your wife."

"That's right."

"But I can be your mistress."

Michael stroked his fingers down her cheek. "Oh, Jensen, you deserve so much more than that."

"I want you. If being your mistress is the only way I can have you, then that's what I want."

"But it's not what I want for you. You deserve to have a man in your life who can be yours and yours alone. You deserve to have children."

"Mistresses have children."

"Illegitimate ones."

"That's not such a stigma in the United States anymore."

"It is in my country."

"Then I'll live in my country if I'm lucky enough to bear a child of yours. We'll see each other whenever we can."

"No. I won't do that to you. I won't allow you to do it to yourself."

"I'll never love anyone else."

Michael kissed her tenderly. "Nor will I."

"Make love to me."

"After what you've just been through…"

"You're leaving tomorrow. This is the last time we'll ever be together. Don't you want to be with me, too?"

Michael didn't say anything. He kissed her long and deep, then rose from the bed, crossed the room to lock the door, then returned to Jensen, stripping off his clothes before lying back on the bed and pulling her into his arms.

He nuzzled her ear. "If I hurt you, tell me."

"Oh," she breathed, "there's nothing you could do that would hurt me."

His mouth moved over her neck and the swell of her breast. His tongue found her nipple and circled it, then he covered it with his mouth and gently sucked.

Jensen couldn't help the moan that escaped her lips.

He wasn't in any hurry as he moved from one breast to the other while his gentle hands moved down her stomach and over her hips, coming back up between her legs and circling his fingers until Jensen was literally writhing.

Then he stopped and raised himself over her, kissing her deeply and letting her feel his desire between her legs without actually entering her.

"Are you all right?" he asked.

"Oh, yes," she breathed as she moved her hands down his body and held him close to her. "I want to touch you," she said as he caught her hand before it reached its mark.

"No." He kissed her more deeply. "One touch from you and I'll be gone."

"Michael."

He kissed his way along her jaw. "What?"

"I want you inside me now."

"Are you sure?"

"Right now."

Michael placed himself directly between her legs and slid himself inside her. "Oh, Lord," he said, "don't move."

Jensen lay completely still, savoring the way it felt to be filled by the man she loved. Her every nerve tingled with desire and expectation.

After a moment, he began moving slowly, in and out.

Jensen had wanted Michael as badly as he'd wanted her. "Michael," she said breathlessly in his ear as she wrapped her legs tightly around him. "I'm not going to last much longer."

He thrust himself inside her up to the hilt, harder and harder, until they both cried out from the sheer agony of the pleasure.

He thrust more slowly and gently as they both came down, then was still.

Jensen held on to him. "Stay inside me," she said against his hear. "Let me just feel you a little longer."

And feel him she did. Within minutes, he filled her again. Jensen began a rhythmic movement with her hips and Michael reacted by meeting her every motion with one of his own of opposite but equal intensity.

She wrapped herself around him, her hands stroking his back, her hips moving with a circular motion.

Within minutes, they were both beyond anything but each other as they exploded again.

Jensen fell weakly back against the pillows. Michael collapsed beside her, pulling her tightly into his arms.

For a long time, neither of them spoke.

Then Michael rested his chin against her forehead. "How am I ever going to let you go now?"

"Don't," she said simply. "I don't care what anyone else thinks of me. I just want to be with you. I just want to have the freedom to love you and be loved by you. Is that too much to ask?"

"I knew we shouldn't have made love. The last thing I want to do is hurt you and that's exactly what I've done."

"No," said Jensen, raising her fingers to his lips. "I wouldn't change what happened between us for the world. If we hadn't, I would have spent the rest of my life wondering what might have been."

"And now?"

"Same question. Different circumstances."

Michael kissed her fingers, then drew her hand away from his lips and kissed her long and tenderly. Pulling her into his arms, he held her close.

"About this mistress thing," she said softly, "you have to let me do it...be it. I can't go through the rest of my life knowing you're somewhere in the world and I'll never see you again."

"Being any man's mistress—particularly a married man's—goes against everything you believe in."

She reached up and cupped his face in her soft

hands. "Michael, I love you so much it hurts. If all you can offer me is the hope of seeing you once in a while, I'll take it."

He pulled her into his arms and held her tight. How, he wondered, could he marry another woman, make love to another woman, have children with another woman, when the only one he'd ever loved—the only one he'd every truly wanted—was half a world away?

"It will tear my heart out when you leave me," he said, "but you will leave. And you will get on with your life."

Jensen choked back a sob. "Please don't do this to us, Michael. Please don't send me away."

Michael pulled her back into his arms and buried his face in her hair. For a long time they just lay there, holding each other.

"I love you," he finally whispered in her ear, "with all my heart and soul. And that's why I have to let you go." He raised his head and looked into her eyes. "You know this."

Jensen gazed into his eyes for a long moment, then touched his cheek with her hand. "I wish you weren't so damned honorable."

Michael managed a half smile. "What happened between us tonight had nothing to do with honor."

"You're not married yet."

His eyes moved over her face; this face he'd never be able to push from his mind. "I think I would have been all right if you hadn't come into my life. I could have managed this marriage."

"Only because you didn't know what love was any more than I did when I came here."

"And now I know." He kissed her gently. "And I almost wish I didn't, because it's going to make the rest of my life a living hell."

Chapter Fifteen

When Jensen walked into her Wisconsin farm-house, it was past midnight. All she had was her backpack, and she dropped that on the floor near the door before walking into the darkened living room and sinking onto the couch.

Her dog would have been with the Shermans at their home down the road.

Henry had gone straight to New York to file his story and meet with his editors before taking a much needed vacation—part of it here with her. He thought she needed the company.

Jensen heard the key in the lock, but didn't move.

"Hello?" called a voice.

"I'm in the living room, Mrs. Sherman," she called back.

Suddenly her dog, a Lab-setter mix, came racing

to her, his tail wagging furiously as he jumped on her with his front paws and tried to lick her anywhere there was exposed flesh.

Jensen laughed for the first time in days and wrapped her arms around her dog's neck. "Oh, Toby, I've missed you."

"He's missed you, too, Jen," said the housekeeper as she stood in the doorway. "Mind if I turn on a light?"

"Go ahead."

She turned on a corner lamp, allowing some gentle light. "How's Henry?"

"Just fine. He asked to be remembered to you, and to warn you that he'll be here in a few days and fully expects to enjoy some of your apple pie."

"I'll make plenty." She took the chair across from Jensen and looked at her closely. "You look dreadful."

Jensen gazed back at her with tired green eyes. "I feel worse than I look. What does that tell you?"

"Want to talk about it?"

Sudden tears filled Jensen's eyes. She dashed them angrily away with the back of her hand. "I'm sorry. I promised myself I was through crying. I've done enough to last a lifetime."

"What happened?"

Jensen scratched the top of Toby's head. "Well, I guess you could say that I just lived out one of my romance novels, but there's no happy ending this time."

"Of course there's a happy ending. Otherwise it's not a proper romance."

"What would you call it when the man you love more than life itself marries another woman."

Mrs. Sherman didn't know what to say.

"Pretty shocking, isn't it?"

"But why?"

"Because honor demands it, and he is nothing if not an honorable man. They're the worst kind, you know. Always doing the right thing. Or trying to. Bastards."

"Oh, my dear, you don't mean that."

Jensen leaned her head back against the couch. "No, of course not. I don't know what to do. I literally don't know what to do. I'm numb inside. I just want to curl up in my bed and stay there."

"It'll pass."

She turned her head to look at the woman who had taken such good care of her for more years than Jensen could remember. "No, it won't, Mrs. Sherman. It will never pass. And that's what makes this so hard. I know this ache inside me is never, ever going to go away, and I haven't figured out how to live with its constant, unending pressure weighing down every breath I take."

"I don't know what to tell you, dear." The woman couldn't have loved Jensen more if she'd been her daughter, and she felt completely helpless in the face of this emotion.

Jensen put the heels of her hands against her eyes and held them there. "I don't think I've ever been so tired."

"Let's get you to bed, then. You go upstairs and

get yourself ready and I'll fix you a little warm milk.''

Jensen didn't say anything for a moment. She didn't want Mrs. Sherman to be upset. Taking her hands away from her eyes, she managed a small smile. "Jet lag is a terrible thing. Just ignore me. What are you doing up at this hour, anyway?''

"Your travel agent called with your schedule. I was waiting up for you.''

Jensen rose, then leaned over and kissed the housekeeper on the cheek. "You are the dearest woman in the world, and I appreciate your care of me. But I don't want any warm milk. I just want my bed. You go on back home to Mr. Sherman where you belong.''

"Are you sure?''

"Very. I'm going to be sound asleep in about five minutes.''

"I can stay in the guest room if you like.''

This time Jensen hugged her. "No. Go home. I'll see you in the morning. Late morning. I plan on sleeping in.''

The woman walked toward the door, still seemingly uncertain.

Jensen managed a bigger smile. "Go on. I'm fine.''

When she'd gone, Jensen dragged herself upstairs to her bedroom. Toby jumped up and lay curled at the foot of the mattress. Jensen rested her cheek against the top of the dog's head, then lay across the bed, fully clothed, shoes still on.

Within minutes, she was sound asleep.

* * *

Michael conducted his business. It was what saved his sanity. As long as he was handling business, he couldn't think about Jensen.

He couldn't remember.

But he still had to deal with nights.

How he hated the darkness.

Sleep was difficult most nights. At other times it was impossible. Every time he closed his eyes, he saw Jensen.

Every time he saw the empty space beside him in his bed, he thought of making love to her; or just holding her.

When he did manage to sleep, he'd reach out for her only to find no one there.

Ali watched him and felt helpless.

Michael did all that was expected of him. More. He went where he was supposed to, met with the dignitaries he had appointments with, said the right things, wrote the right letters—but it was as though he was in a constant state of grieving and there was nothing that could relieve it. Not for a single moment.

He hadn't smiled since Jensen had left.

The light had gone from his eyes.

There was even some gray in his hair that hadn't been there before. It was distinguished looking, but he was far too young to have it.

One day, Ali knocked on Michael's office door and walked in.

Michael looked up from what he was doing.

"I think it's time for a trip to the desert, Your Highness."

"I appreciate the thought, Ali, but there's too much to be done."

"Please, take my advice on this. I have the horses ready and the gear packed. Your calendar is clear. All that's needed is you."

Michael looked at his desk. "Give me an hour."

Ali inclined his head. "Yes, sir. I'll be waiting."

Michael finished what he was doing, changed into desert clothes and went out to find Ali standing by with two horses.

Without speaking, Michael climbed on his and the two men took off at full gallop, riding for hours in the early evening and stopping only to water the horses.

When they arrived at their destination—the tent where he'd spent the night with Jensen—Michael dismounted, handed the reins to Ali and climbed up the dune to sit with his legs crossed and watch while the sun set over the sand.

When Ali had finished rubbing down the horses and getting them ready for the night, he climbed the dune and sat beside Michael. Their relationship was abnormally informal since Jensen had come into their lives.

And left.

"You're not taking care of yourself," said Ali.

"I'm doing the best I can."

"Is it your Jensen?"

Michael didn't say anything for a moment. "Every day without her is like a new torture."

"Then you need to be with her."

"I can't."

"I didn't say you had to marry her."

"That's what she said. In fact, she offered to be my mistress. Even to bear my children."

"And you sent her away?"

"I couldn't do that to her."

"Do you think she's any happier than you are at this moment?"

"No," Michael said. "I think we are probably very much equal in our misery."

"Then what's the point?"

"You met her, Ali. You got to know her. This isn't the kind of woman who spends her life as some man's mistress."

"Not under ordinary circumstances. But she happened to fall in love with you. And you are not just some man. You would marry her if you could, but you can't. She knows this and still she wants to be with you. Doesn't that count for anything?"

"Do you think it was easy for me to send her away?"

"No. I saw your face when you were told she'd gone. I think it was one of the most difficult things you've ever done. And I think it was a mistake."

Michael let out a long breath.

"I saw her face, too. Something you did not."

Michael said nothing.

"I think it was a mistake. If ever two people were meant to be together, it's you and Jensen. However you have to manage it. However few the days or short the hours, you need each other to survive. I can see that, and I'm not all that observant when it comes to human nature. Surely you must feel it.''

"I die a little inside every day that I'm not with her," Michael said.

"Then set aside everything you think you believe to be true, everything you think is right and proper, and know that the only thing that matters is being with this woman."

"I don't know if I can do that."

"You think you're making a great sacrifice for her by not allowing her to be your mistress. You're keeping your honor and allowing her to keep hers. But what if the only thing that's being sacrificed is Jensen herself? How can you want her to suffer the way you are? If there's a way for you to both be happy—at least some of the time—then don't you owe it to her as well as to yourself to seize the opportunity?"

Ali rose from the sand.

"I've said my piece. Now, I'll leave you with your thoughts."

"Ali?"

"Yes, Your Highness?"

"Thank you. You're a good friend."

"I try to be. But you make it difficult at times."

A corner of Michael's mouth lifted. "She hates the desert, you know."

"It's a difficult adjustment for anyone." Ali touched his king's shoulder. "Good night."

"Good night, Ali."

As the silence of the desert fell around him, Michael stayed where he was and stared at the night sky with its dusting of stars.

Jensen.

Jensen stared at her computer screen.

Nothing.

There wasn't a story in her.

Not a chapter.

Not a paragraph.

Not a sentence.

It was as though every emotion had been wrung from her.

Mrs. Sherman came in with a plateful of cookies and a glass of milk. "Time for a break."

Jensen looked at the plate and shook her head. "I feel like I'm twelve again."

"You might as well be, the way you've been mooning around here, not writing, not eating. You're growing thinner by the day. You need to get some calories into yourself."

"I eat."

"When I force you."

Jensen took a cookie from the plate and took a bite. "See?"

"Eat the whole thing and drink the milk."

"Then will you leave me alone?" Jensen asked, a kind edge to her voice.

"For a little while."

Jensen took another bite of cookie and turned off her computer. "It's no use. I have nothing to say."

"But you have file drawers full of ideas."

"I know. But I seem to have forgotten how to tell the stories. Or lost the will."

"You just need time." She pressed the glass of milk into Jensen's hand and watched while she drank it.

Just to make the housekeeper happy, Jensen drank it all and handed her back the glass.

"Another cookie?" asked Mrs. Sherman as she offered the plate. "They're your favorite."

Jensen took another.

"Good girl. You'll see. Everything will be fine in no time."

Mrs. Sherman was convinced that cookies and milk could fix anything, no matter how old you were.

As soon as she'd gone, Jensen set the cookie on her desk and walked to the window. It was a beautiful fall day. Too beautiful to be sitting in her office.

Not bothering with a sweater or jacket, Jensen left the house through the back entrance and headed into her woods, Toby by her side.

Mrs. Sherman saw her from the kitchen window and shook her head. The girl was wasting away.

As the housekeeper finished the dishes, there was a knock on the front door.

She opened it, a dish towel in her hands, to find a remarkably handsome young man standing there in what was probably a hideously expensive suit. "Is Jensen here?"

Mrs. Sherman didn't give out information to anyone unless there was a good reason. "Who wants to know?"

"I'm Michael Hassan."

She suddenly clutched his arm. "You're her Michael?"

"Is she here?"

"She went for a walk in the woods. You can catch her if you walk fast."

"What direction?" asked Michael.

The housekeeper pointed. "She usually makes for a small pond about a mile in."

"Thank you." He indicated the man behind him. It was the first time the housekeeper had noticed him. "This is Ali, my bodyguard. Would you mind if he waited for me in the house?"

Mrs. Sherman looked him up and down. "You're a pretty scary looking fellow," she said bluntly.

Ali said nothing.

"He'll grow on you," said Michael.

She gave him another once-over. "I suppose you can wait inside, but don't be talking to me. I have work to do."

Ali took up a stance inside the front door, his legs apart, his arms behind his back and his sword very much in evidence.

Michael took off down the stairs and ran into the woods after Jensen.

He stopped once and called her name, but there was no answer.

He walked quickly, brightly colored leaves crunching under his feet, the fall sunlight creating a dappled effect on the forest floor.

And then he saw her.

She had stopped by the pond and lain down in the leaves, her hands behind her head.

Toby saw Michael first and ran over to him, tail wagging. Michael ran his hand over the dog's back, but his focus was Jensen.

She didn't see him until he was perhaps five feet away. And even then she didn't believe it. She just stared at him, then raised up on her elbows. "Michael?"

He knelt beside her and pulled her into his arms with a groan that came from someplace deep within. Jensen wrapped her arms around him and buried her face in his neck—that wonderful smelling neck—afraid to speak for fear that he'd disappear.

"I didn't think I'd ever get here," he said as he held her away and looked into her eyes.

"Why are you?"

"I can't breathe without you."

Jensen's eyes filled with tears as she reached out and touched the gray in his hair. "Look at you."

"I want you in my life, Jensen. Whatever the terms. If you can live with them, I can."

"You mean I'm going to be a sheik's mistress?"

"I'd rather have you as my wife, but since that's not possible, mistress is the best I can do."

Jensen wrapped her arms around his neck. "Don't you know that I'll take you any way I can get you?"

"That's what Ali said."

"He's a wise man. I always suspected as much."

"I don't want to hurt you."

"Not being with you hurts me. Not seeing you or

talking to you hurts me. If I can just have you some-times, I can live with the pain the rest of the time.''

Michael touched her hair. "You may be stronger than I am.''

She pulled him down onto the carpet of leaves with her. "There's no one around. Even Toby's dis-appeared.''

"Toby?''

"My dog.''

Michael unzipped his trousers while Jensen pulled down her jeans. A moment later Michael disap-peared inside her. They both climaxed almost in-stantly and with ferocious intensity.

Michael wrapped her in his arms and held her as close as a man can hold a woman.

"How long do I have you for?'' she asked.

"I leave tomorrow afternoon. My wedding is in three days.''

The last words were like a knife, but she handled them. "Then let's not waste a single moment. I want to know every thought you've had since I left you, everything you've done, every word you've ut-tered…''

"You don't ask much, do you?''

"Let's go back to the house.''

"Ali is there with your housekeeper.''

Jensen couldn't help smiling as she pulled up her jeans. "Ali and Mrs. Sherman. Now there's an in-teresting combination.''

"When I left them, Mrs. Sherman appeared to have the upper hand.''

"I'm not surprised.''

"Where can we go to be alone? I don't want to share you with anyone for the short time I'm going to be here," Michael said.

"I'll send Mrs. Sherman home early, and Ali can stay in the guest house. It's not very big, but it's comfortable. It's where Henry stays when he visits."

Michael looked at her and smiled.

"What?"

"I can't tell you how happy it makes me just to look at you."

Jensen got to her feet and held out her hand to pull Michael to his. They walked back to the house hand in hand, happy at last, Toby running ahead of them.

When they got to the house, Mrs. Sherman was in the kitchen finishing up. Ali was in the living room eating cookies and drinking milk. Without thinking about protocol, she ran across the room to him and flung herself into his arms.

Ali folded her into them and hugged her. "It's nice to see you, miss."

"And you," Jensen said as she pulled away and looked into his eyes. "I understand I owe you thanks for this."

"He would have made the right decision eventually. I only helped him along."

She kissed his cheek. "Thank you."

Jensen was glowing as she walked into the kitchen and the housekeeper couldn't help but smile. "Well," she said, "this is a change of circumstance."

"You'll be happy to know, Mrs. Sherman," said

Jensen, "that you have off until the day after to-morrow. I'd appreciate it if you'd show Ali to the guest house on your way out and make sure he has everything he needs to last him until tomorrow afternoon."

The housekeeper looked directly at Michael. "You make sure she eats."

"I will."

Neatly folding the dish towel, she put it on the rack and went to the living room to get Ali. "And I'll take Toby with me," she called over her shoulder.

When they'd gone, Michael went upstairs to shower. Jensen built a fire in the living room, then went upstairs, stripped off her clothes and stepped into the shower with Michael where they made love again under the softly running water, this time more slowly.

"Oh, Jensen," he sighed against her ear as the water ran over their bodies, "will I ever stop wanting you?"

"I hope not."

When they dried off, Jensen put on a long-tailed shirt and nothing else. Michael put on jeans and left his chest bare.

It was dark in the house except for the flickering of the fire as they sat on a blanket in front of it, sipping their wine. Or, rather, Michael was sipping wine. Jensen was sipping mineral water.

"I like your Wisconsin," said Michael. "It's beautiful. So full of color. And the air is crisp. Clean."

"Especially this time of year," said Jensen. "Personally I think it's even prettier when it's green."

"It's a good place to raise children."

"I think so."

He turned his head to look at her. "I want to have children with you."

"Do you mean that?"

"With all my heart."

"Then congratulations, because you're going to be a father."

"What?"

"It happened the first night we were together. I'm six weeks pregnant."

Michael touched her face in wonder. "How long have you known?"

"I think, in my heart, I knew that night. But I wasn't sure until a few weeks ago."

"Were you going to tell me?"

"I hadn't decided yet. Probably not."

"You would have gone through it alone?"

"You had your own things to deal with. I didn't want to add to your burdens."

"A child with you is no burden. It's a joy."

Jensen thought she saw something on his face in the firelight. She reached up in wonder and touched his cheek. "A tear?"

He caught her hand and brought her palm to his lips, holding it there. "I wish we could raise the baby together."

"I know. But you'll see it sometimes."

"Not as a true parent should."

"I'll tell him or her all about you. I'll show the

child pictures so it knows who you are. And when you're here, we'll be a family. A real family.''

''We'll talk every day,'' he said. ''And I want to be with you for the birth.''

''Thank you. You have no idea how much I want you to be a part of that.''

He pulled her into his arms and held her.

Three days.

Three days and he would be married to another woman.

Chapter Sixteen

It was the day before his wedding. Michael was sitting in his office, staring into space. All he could think about was Jensen.

His secretary knocked on his door and entered, closing it behind him and looking distressed.

"What is it?" he asked the man.

"Your fiancée's father is here to see you."

"Sheik Mommar?"

"Yes. And he has no appointment."

"It doesn't matter. Show him in." Michael prepared himself to take it on the chin. The man must have found out about his trip to be with Jensen.

He rose as the older man was shown in.

Right away, Michael knew he'd misjudged the purpose of the visit. This wasn't an angry sheik trying to make things right for his daughter. This was a devastated man.

Michael quickly crossed the room and put his hand on his shoulder. "What is it?"

He handed Michael a note. "This will explain everything."

Michael unfolded it and read the words he'd hardly dared to hope for. Ayalah had eloped to France with the man she loved. There was to be no marriage with Michael.

It was all he could do not to shout for joy as he crumpled the letter in his hand.

The older man misunderstood the younger man's emotion and nodded his head. "I don't know what to say. This is the greatest insult. This is not how she was raised. Her mother and I..." His eyes filled with tears. "She is dead to us, of course."

"No, no, please," said Michael, leading the man to a chair and pressing him into it. "Don't do that."

"We have no choice. She has disgraced us all."

"Ayalah was to be my wife, and I find no disgrace in what she has done. She loved another man and went to be with him. Please, don't punish her for that."

The older man looked up at Michael in confusion. "But the agreement with your father has been broken. Our two families were to be united through this marriage."

"Yes," said Michael. "And my father is dead. He, as much as anyone, would understand what your daughter did. He, too, married for love."

"I have a younger daughter," suggested the man,

rising. "She would be more than willing to step into her sister's shoes. The same royal blood runs through her veins."

"No, no, please," said Michael. "Consider this matter ended here and now, with no harsh feelings between our families. And I hope none toward your daughter and her new husband. I would be very disappointed to find out that you had rejected her."

The man shook Michael's hand. "I'm relieved that you're taking this so well. If ever you need anything, know that you have a friend."

"Thank you."

As soon as the man had left, Michael buzzed his secretary.

"Yes, sir?"

"The wedding is off. Cancel all of the plans. And I want my jet readied for a trip to the United States."

"To leave when?"

"Immediately."

"But you were just there."

"And I'm going back. Now do it."

"Yes, sir. Is there anyone there who should be notified? Any officials?"

"No one."

When they arrived at Jensen's house, it was past midnight. Ali waited in the car while Michael rang the bell.

Jensen was lying in bed, but she wasn't asleep. In Sumaruan time, Michael—her Michael—was marrying another woman.

When the doorbell rang, she sat up with a frown. Who could that be?

Then she smiled. Henry, of course.

She padded barefoot downstairs, Toby by her side, turning on a light as she went, and opened the door.

Her lips parted softly when she saw the man standing there. "Michael? What are you doing here?"

He lifted her off her feet and held her in his arms. "I'm free. Ayalah ran off with her lover." He set her down. "Get dressed. We're getting married."

"Now?"

"This minute. I called ahead and made the arrangements."

"But I don't have a proper dress...."

He touched her cheek, his heart in his eyes. "We'll have a formal wedding another time. Right now, I just want to be married to you. Wear jeans, for all I care."

Jensen couldn't believe what she was hearing. She threw her arms around his neck and held on for dear life. "I can't believe this is happening. I'm so afraid I'm going to wake up and find this is all just a dream."

Michael picked her up and carried her into the house and up the stairs to her room, setting her down in front of her closet. "Get dressed. Mr. and Mrs. Sherman are waiting. And Henry will be attending by satellite phone."

While Michael sat on the bed and watched, Jensen pulled out a white dress with long sleeves and a skirt that flared midthigh. She put it on, along with high heels, and turned to Michael. "What do you think?"

"That you're the most beautiful woman in the world."

Jensen went to the bed and kissed him. "I think I could wear a potato sack and you'd still think I was beautiful."

"I look at you, not what you're wearing."

She sat at her old-fashioned dressing table and put on a little makeup, but when she started to brush her hair, Michael took it from her and began running it through the silken strands in long, slow strokes.

"Should I leave it down?"

"Yes," he answered simply, putting the brush back on the dresser. "Now, let's go."

"Where?"

Ali was on the porch when they came out. He smiled at her and inclined his head.

She smiled back, still confused.

As soon as they went around to the back of the house, Jensen saw that someone had been busy. Lights had been strung along the path she took to the pond, showing them the way.

Jensen wasn't used to walking over the uneven ground in high heels. She lost her balance and again Michael swept her into his arms and carried her the rest of the way to the pond where Mr. and Mrs. Sherman both waited with a black-robed judge.

Michael set Jensen down in front of her and handed Jensen a phone.

"Henry?" said Jensen.

"So you're really going to do it," came his cheerful voice. "I can't believe my little sister is getting married."

"Where are you?"

"Zaire. I'll be back in a few weeks."

"I've heard that one before."

Henry laughed. "Look, get on with it, will you? The connection is bad and getting worse. I want to hear this."

She handed the phone back to Mr. Sherman, who moved next to the judge and held it out so Henry could hear.

Mrs. Sherman handed her a bouquet of fall flowers from her own garden and kissed her cheek. "A happy ending," she said. "I guess this is a romance after all."

And then the judge was speaking.

Jensen heard herself making all the right responses, but her own voice seemed to come from a distance.

Mostly she looked into Michael's eyes. The love she saw there filled her completely.

She let him slip a ring onto her finger.

Then Ali handed her a ring to put on Michael's finger.

And it was done.

Henry offered his crackling congratulations just as the connection was lost.

Michael held her in his arms. "Now we're complete," he said.

Tears streamed down Jensen's cheeks.

He smiled as he gently wiped them away. "You cry more than any woman I've ever met."

"I hope you find it one of my more endearing qualities, because you're going to be seeing a lot of them over the years."

"I find all of your qualities endearing. Even your temper."

She reached up and touched his face, still in wonder at what had happened. "I can't believe we can really be together. Your people..."

"Will learn to love you."

"You say that with such certainty."

"When they know you, as they will come to over the years, they will love you. No one who meets you can resist. Ali is proof of that."

"Can I still write my novels?"

"Of course."

"And can I keep my home here so we can visit sometimes?"

"I wouldn't have it any other way. I want our children to know both sides of their heritage and treasure them equally."

"Oh, Michael," she said with a sigh, "I love you."

Epilogue

Jensen gave a final push and out came the most perfect baby boy she'd ever seen—or heard. His lusty cries filled the room.

Michael looked at his son, and then at his wife, and for the second time since knowing him, Jensen saw his eyes fill with tears.

He pulled Jensen into his arms. "Are you all right?"

"Oh, yes." She was almost laughing with relief. It was over.

"I can't believe what you went through."

"All woman do."

He kissed her perspiration-damp hair and straightened away from her only when the nurse handed her their new son, already swaddled in a light blanket.

He leaned over the child and looked into the tiny face.

Jensen touched the soft little cheek.

Michael leaned over and gathered them both in his arms, then took Jensen's hand and raised it to his lips, as he gazed at her.

"We'll never make our son marry a woman he doesn't love, will we?" she asked.

"Never."

"And if he doesn't want to be a king...?"

Michael leaned over and kissed her lips. "Perhaps by that time our little country will be a democracy."

"Oh, Michael," she whispered, "I love you. Just when I think I couldn't possibly love you more, I find I do."

He kissed her again.

The look in his eyes said it all.

* * * * *

MATERNITY LEAVE

Coming September 1998

Three delightful stories about the blessings
and surprises of "Labor" Day.

TABLOID BABY by Candace Camp

She was whisked to the hospital in the nick of time....

THE NINE-MONTH KNIGHT
by Cait London

A down-on-her-luck secretary is experiencing
odd little midnight cravings....

THE PATERNITY TEST by Sherryl Woods

The stick turned blue before her
biological clock struck twelve....

*These three special women are very pregnant...and very
single, although they won't be either for too much longer,
because baby—and Daddy—are on their way!*

Available at your favorite retail outlet.

Take 2 bestselling love stories FREE

Plus get a FREE surprise gift!

Special Limited-Time Offer

Mail to Silhouette Reader Service™

3010 Walden Avenue
P.O. Box 1867
Buffalo, N.Y. 14240-1867

YES! Please send me 2 free Silhouette Special Edition® novels and my free surprise gift. Then send me 6 brand-new novels every month, which I will receive months before they appear in bookstores. Bill me at the low price of $3.57 each plus 25¢ delivery and applicable sales tax, if any.* That's the complete price, and a saving of over 10% off the cover prices—quite a bargain! I understand that accepting the books and gift places me under no obligation ever to buy any books. I can always return a shipment and cancel at any time. Even if I never buy another book from Silhouette, the 2 free books and the surprise gift are mine to keep forever.

235 SEN CH7W

Name	(PLEASE PRINT)	
Address	Apt. No.	
City	State	Zip

This offer is limited to one order per household and not valid to present Silhouette Special Edition® subscribers. *Terms and prices are subject to change without notice. Sales tax applicable in N.Y.

USPED-98   ©1990 Harlequin Enterprises Limited

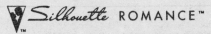

Silhouette® SPECIAL EDITION®

Newfound sisters Bliss, Tiffany and Katie
learn more about family and true love
than they *ever* expected.

A new miniseries by

LISA JACKSON

A FAMILY KIND OF GUY (SE#1191) August 1998
Bliss Cawthorne wanted nothing to do with ex-flame
Mason Lafferty, the cowboy who had destroyed her
dreams of being his bride. Could Bliss withstand his irresistible charm—the second time around?

A FAMILY KIND OF GAL (SE#1207) November 1998
How could widowed single mother Tiffany Santini be
attracted to her sexy brother-in-law, J.D.? Especially
since J.D. was hiding something that could destroy the
love she had just found in his arms....

And watch for the conclusion of this series in
early 1999 with Katie Kinkaid's story in
A FAMILY KIND OF WEDDING.

Available at your favorite retail outlet. Only from

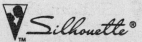
Silhouette®

Look us up on-line at: http://www.romance.net

SSEHCTB